Praise for the fiction of Leonard Michaels

"Slapstick, even the neurotic slapstick of [Philip] Roth, is too tame for Michaels's dark vision. In his fiction, bodies are not just teased by sex; they are mocked and distorted, as savagely as in a Bosch triptych . . . The more outlandishly transgressive Michaels's writing becomes, the more intensely the reader senses his nostalgia for the humane . . . [Michaels] makes genuine drama out of the life of the mind [and] fireworks out of the ordeals of the body." —Adam Kirsch, *The New York Sun*

"*The Collected Stories* . . . is frankly startling in its talent, energy, sensitivity, and savagery." —Frances Reade, *SF Weekly*

"Larky, fitfully brilliant, as profane as they are aphoristic, Leonard Michaels's stories stand alongside those of his best Jewish contemporaries—Grace Paley and Philip Roth . . . To be read again and again."

—Mona Simpson, *The New York Times Book Review*

"[Michaels] could sound absurdist like Donald Barthelme one day, and, the next, like a Beat poet . . . Whether he was writing a classic story or a memoirlike vignette, his style seemed free and easy." —Troy Patterson, *Entertainment Weekly*

"Written in a style outwardly calmer than the snap and crackle of his earlier stories with their sentences that explode like cluster bombs, the Nachman stories are nevertheless just as tensile, disturbing and unpredictable."

—Stanley Fish, *The New York Times*

"What was the *music* inside these stories? How was it done? It was a different way of listening, seeing and, ultimately, assembling. The stories—some as short as three lines, others pared down to a sharp volley of dialogue—were full of beautiful, glinting sentences, details laid on like pigment on canvas. [Michaels's] first sentences made you want to eavesdrop."

—Lynell George, *Los Angeles Times*

"The best writer I [have] ever encountered . . . The writer who influences me more than any other."

—David Bezmozgis, *Nextbook*

"*The Collected Stories* . . . argue[s] effortlessly for a place beside the work of America's paragons of the story form."

—Wyatt Mason, *Harper's Magazine*

"[Michaels's] prose moved at a fast clip and paid readers the compliment of assuming they could match his mental velocity, with a concise, pungent and pyrotechnic style that tolerated no flab . . . The publication of his collected stories should win him many new fans, offering as it does ample proof that he was among the few essential American short story writers of the past half-century . . . [*Sylvia*,] about a hideous start-up bohemian marriage in Greenwich Village, is one of the most powerful pieces of autobiographical prose to have resulted from this age of the memoir." —Philip Lopate, *The Nation*

"Michaels, it seems, never wrote a boring sentence."
—Barbara Fisher, *The Boston Globe*

"From the 1960s until his death in 2003, Michaels buzzed through a variety of modes—surrealism, interior monologue, essay-tale, traditional narrative. *The Collected Stories* would make an admirable master class in the art of short fiction if its brilliance weren't likely to drive aspiring writers to despair . . . Close to perfection . . . It's dazzling, it's outlandish."
—Craig Seligman, *Newsday*

"Wondrous, mad, instructive and disabusing, [Michaels's work] should be widely read." —Joshua Cohen, *Forward*

"[Michaels] wrote with humor and a Yiddish verve that could only be so riotously blasphemous because it's tethered to the sacred culture of the Old Country. Leonard Michaels should never be put on the same pedestal as Phillip Roth and Grace Paley. He was unique; he deserves his own."

—Daniel Septimus, *The Jerusalem Post*

"Unexpected outcomes flourish. Illogic is forced into coherence and sense by the power of the prose . . . Pitch-perfect humor, cutting and witty . . . retrieves these stories from the brink of nihilism." —Kevin Doughten, *The Bloomsbury Review*

By Leonard Michaels

Time Out of Mind: The Diaries of Leonard Michaels, 1961–1995

A Girl with a Monkey

To Feel These Things

Sylvia

Shuffle

The Men's Club

I Would Have Saved Them If I Could

Going Places

Edited by Leonard Michaels

West of the West: Imagining California
(with David Reid and Raquel Scherr)

The State of the Language (with Christopher Ricks)

THE
MEN'S CLUB

THE

MEN'S CLUB

THE

MEN'S CLUB

Leonard Michaels

Farrar, Straus and Giroux

18 West 18th Street, New York 10011

Copyright © 1978, 1981 by Leonard Michaels

All rights reserved

Distributed in Canada by Douglas & McIntyre Ltd.

Printed in the United States of America

Originally published in 1981 by Farrar, Straus and Giroux

Library of Congress Control Number 2007940158

Hardcover ISBN-13: 978-0-374-20819-6

Paperback ISBN-10: 0-374-20819-0

Designed by Cynthia Krupat

Farrar, Straus and Giroux

NEW YORK

4   5   7   9   10   8   6   4

Farrar, Straus and Giroux
18 West 18th Street, New York 10011

Distributed in Canada by Douglas & McIntyre Ltd.
Printed in the United States of America
Originally published in 1981 by Farrar, Straus and Giroux

Library of Congress Control Number: 2007940458
Paperback ISBN-13: 978-0-374-20819-6
Paperback ISBN-10: 0-374-20819-0

Designed by Cynthia Krupat

www.fsgbooks.com

3   5   7   9   10   8   6   4

For Brenda

THE

MEN'S CLUB

Women wanted to talk about anger, identity, politics, etc. I saw posters in Berkeley urging them to join groups. I saw their leaders on TV. Strong, articulate faces. So when Cavanaugh phoned and invited me to join a men's club, I laughed. Slowly, not laughing, he repeated himself. He was six foot nine. The size and weight entered his voice. He and some friends wanted a club. "A regular social possibility outside of our jobs and marriages. Nothing to do with women's groups." One man was a tax accountant, another was a lawyer. There was also a college teacher like me and two psychotherapists. Solid types. I supposed there could be virtues in a men's club, a regular social possibility. I should have said yes immediately, but something in me resisted. The prospect of leaving my house after dinner to go to a meeting. Blood is heavy then. Brain is slow. Besides, wasn't this club idea corny? Like trying to recapture high-school days. Locker-room fun. Wet naked boys snapping towels at each other's genitals. It didn't feel exactly right. To be wretchedly truthful, any social possibility unrelated to wife, kids, house, and work felt like a form of adultery. Not criminal. Not legitimate.

"Cavanaugh, I don't even go to the movies anymore."

"I'm talking about a men's club. Good company. You talk about women's groups. Movies. Can't you hear me?"

"When the phone rings, it's like an attack on my life. I get confused. Say it again."

"Listen to me, man. You're one of my best friends. You live less than a mile away, but do we see each other three times a year? When is the last time we talked to each other, really talked?"

"I lose over a month a year just working to pay property taxes. Friendship is a luxury. Unless you're so poor it makes no difference how you spend your time."

"A men's club. Good company."

"I hear you."

But I was thinking about good company. Some of my married colleagues had love affairs, usually with students. You could call it a regular social possibility. It included emotional chaos. Gonorrhea. Even guilt. They would have been better off in a men's club.

"What do you say? Can we expect you?"

"I'll go to the first meeting. I can't promise more. I'm very busy."

"Yeah, yeah," said Cavanaugh and gave me an address in the Berkeley flats. A man named Harry Kramer lived there. I was to look for a redwood fence and pine trees.

The night of the meeting I told my wife I'd be home early. Before midnight, certainly. I had to teach the next day. She said, "Take out the garbage." Big sticky bag felt unpropitious and my hands soon smelled of tuna fish. After driving only five minutes, I found the place.

The front of the house, vine-covered, seemed to brood in lunatic privacy. Nobody answered when I knocked, but I heard voices, took hold of a wrought-iron handle and pushed, discovering a large Berkeley living room and five men inside. I saw dark wood paneling and potted ferns dangling from exposed beams. Other plants along the window ledges. A potted tree in a far corner, skinny, spinsterish-looking. Nervous yellow leaves filled its head. Various ceramics, bowls on tabletops and plates on the walls beside large acrylic paintings, abstractions like glistening viscera splashed off a butcher block. Also an amazing rug, but I couldn't take it in. A man was rising from a pillow, coming toward me, smiling.

"I knocked," I said.

"Come in, man. I'm Harry Kramer."

"I'm Cavanaugh's friend."

"Who isn't?"

"Really," I said, giving it the L.A. inflection to suggest sympathetic understanding, not wonder. Kramer registered the nuance and glanced at me as at a potential brother.

His heavy black hair was controlled by a style, parted in the middle and shaped to cup his ears in a way that once belonged to little girls. It was contradicted by black force in his eyes, handshake like a bite, and tattooed forearms. Blue, winged snake. Blue dagger amid roses. They spoke for an earlier life, I supposed, but Kramer wore his sleeves rolled to the elbow. It was hard to connect him with his rug, which I began to appreciate as spongy and orange. I felt myself wading and bouncing through it as Kramer led me toward the men.

Shaking hands, nodding hello, saying my name, each man was a complex flash——eyes, hand, name ——but one had definition. He was graphic; instantly closer to me than the others. Solly Berliner. Tall, skinny, wearing a suit. Dead-white hair and big greenish light in his eyes. The face of an infant surprised by senility. His suit was gray polyester, conservative and sleazy. Kramer left me with Berliner beside the potted tree, a beer in my hand. A man about five foot six or seven came right up to us. "Care for a taste?" In his palm lay two brown marijuanas, slick with spittle. I declined. Berliner said, "Thanks, thanks," with frightening gratitude, and took both cigarettes. We laughed. Then he dropped one back into the man's palm. Turning toward the others, the man said, "Anyone care for a taste?"

The sound of Berliner's voice lingered after the joke; loud, impulsive. Maybe he felt uneasy. Out of his natural environment. I couldn't guess where that might be. He was a confusion of clues. The suit wasn't Berkeley. The eyes were worlds of feeling. His speedy voice flew from nerves. Maybe the living room affected him. A men's club would have seemed more authentic, more properly convened, elsewhere. What did I have in mind? A cold ditch? I supposed Kramer's wife, exiled for the evening, had cultivated

7

the plants and picked the orange rug and the luscious
fabrics on the couches and chairs. Ideas of happiness.
Berliner and I remained standing, as if the fabrics—
heavy velvets, beige tones—were nothing to violate
with our behinds. It was a woman's living room, but so
what? The point of the club was to be with men, not
to worry about women. I turned to Berliner and asked
what he did for a living.

"Real estate," he said, grinning ferociously, as if
extreme types were into that. Wild fellows. "I drove
in from San Jose." He spoke with rapid little shrugs,
as if readjusting his vertebrae. His eyes, after two
drags on the cigarette, were full of green distance. He
was already driving back to San Jose, I figured. Then
he said, "Forgive me for saying this, but a minute ago,
when Kramer introduced us, I had a weird thought."

"You did?"

His eyes returned to me with a look I'd seen before.
It signaled the California plunge into truth.

"I hope this doesn't bother you. I thought . . ."

I waited.

"Oh, forget it, man."

"No, please go on. What did you think?"

"I thought you had a withered leg."

"You did?"

"Yeah, but I see you don't. Isn't that weird?"

"Weird that I don't have a withered leg?"

"Yeah, I thought your leg was all screwed up. Like withered."

I wiggled my legs. For my sake, not his. He stared as if into unusual depths and seemed, regardless of my wiggling, not convinced. Then he said, "I'm forty-seven."

"You look much younger." This was true. But, with the white hair, he also looked older.

"I stay in shape," he answered, marijuana smoke leaking from his nostrils. "Nobody," he said, sucking the leak back against crackling sheets of snot, "nobody else in the room is forty-seven. I'm oldest. I asked the guys."

He gagged, then released smoke, knifing it through compressed lips. "Kramer is thirty-eight."

I wondered if conversation had ever been more like medical experience, so rich in gas and mucus. "I'm always the oldest. Ever since I was a kid I was the oldest." He giggled and intensified his stare, waiting for me to confess something, too. I giggled back at him in a social way. Then the door opened and Cavanaugh walked in.

"Excuse me," I said, intimating regret but moving quickly away.

My friend Cavanaugh—big, handsome guy—had

heroic charisma. He'd been a professional basketball player. Now he worked at the university in special undergraduate programs, matters of policy and funding. Nine to five, jacket and tie. To remember his former work—the great naked shoulders and legs flying through the air—was saddening. In restaurants and airports people still asked for his autograph.

Things felt better, more natural, healthier, with the big man in the room. Kramer reached him before I did. They slapped each other's arms, laughing, pleased at how they felt to each other. Solid. Real. I watched, thinking I'd often watched Cavanaugh. Ever since college, in fact, when he'd become famous. To see him burn his opponent and score was like a miracle of justice. In civilian clothes, he was faintly disorienting. Especially his wristwatch, a golden, complicated band. Symbolic manacle. Cavanaugh's submission to ordinary life. He didn't burn anybody. He'd once said, "I don't want my kids to grow up like me, necks thicker than their heads." He wanted his kids in jackets and wristwatches.

He stopped slapping Kramer's arms, but Kramer continued touching him and looked as though he might soon pee in his pants. People love athletes. Where else these days do they see such mythic drama? Images of unimpeachable excellence. I was infected by

Kramer's enthusiasm, a bit giddy now at the sight of Cavanaugh. When Kramer left to get him a beer, we shook hands. He said, "I didn't think I'd see you tonight." There was mockery in his smile.

"It's not so easy getting out of the house. Nobody but you could have dragged me to this."

"You open the door, you're out."

"Tell me about it."

"I'm glad you're here. Anything happen yet? I'm a little late because Sarah thinks the club idea is wrong. I'm wrong to be here. We argued at dinner." He whispered, "Maybe it isn't easy," and looked at his wristwatch, frowning, as if it were his mind. Kramer returned with the beer just as a phone started ringing.

"I'll be right back," said Kramer, turning to the ringing.

Sarah's word "wrong" seemed wrong to me. If something was wrong with Cavanaugh, it was wrong with the universe. Men could understand that. When Cavanaugh needed a loan to buy his house, the bank gave him no trouble. You could see his credit was good; he was six foot nine and could run a hundred yards in ten seconds. The loan officer, a man, recognized Cavanaugh and didn't even ask about his recent divorce or alimony payments.

Men's clubs. Women's groups. They suggest incur-
able disorders. I remembered Socrates—how the boys,
not his wife, adored him. And Karl Marx running
around with Engels while Jenny stayed home with the
kids. Maybe men played more than women. A men's
club, compared to women's groups, was play. Friv-
olous; virtually insulting. It excluded women. But I
was thinking in circles. A men's club didn't exclude
women. It also didn't exclude kangaroos. It included
only men. I imagined explaining this to Sarah. "You
see, men love to play." It didn't feel convincing. She
had strong opinions and a bad temper. When Cavanaugh quit basketball, it was his decision, but I
blamed her anyway. She wanted him home. The king
became the dean.

Kramer shouted from another room, "Is anybody
here named Terry? His wife is on the phone. She's
crying." Shouting again, more loudly, as if to make
sure the woman on the phone would hear him, Kramer
said, "Is anybody in this house named Terry?"

Nobody admitted to being named Terry.

Shouting again, Kramer said, "Terry isn't here. If
Terry shows up, I'll tell him to phone you right away.
No, I won't forget."

When Kramer returned he said, "You guys sure
none of you is named Terry?"

Cavanaugh muttered, "We're all named Terry. Let's get this club started."

We made a circle, some of us sitting on the rug on pillows. Kramer began talking in a slow, rational voice. The black eyes darkened his face. His words became darker, heavier, because of them.

"What is the purpose of this club?"

To make women cry, I thought. Kramer's beginning was not very brilliant, but he looked so deep that I resisted judgment.

"Some of us—Solly Berliner, Paul, Cavanaugh— had a discussion a few weeks ago. We agreed it would be a good idea . . ."

Paul was the short, marijuana man; he had an eager face and voice. Kramer nodded to him when he said his name. He went on about the good idea. I wasn't listening.

I thought again about the women. Anger, identity, politics, rights, wrongs. I envied them. It seemed attractive to be deprived in our society. Deprivation gives you something to fight for, it makes you morally superior, it makes you serious. What was left for men these days? They already had everything. Did they need clubs? The mere sight of two men together suggests a club. Consider Damon and Pythias, Huck and Jim, Hamlet and Horatio. The list is familiar. Even the Lone Ranger wasn't lonely. He had Tonto. There is Gertrude Stein and Alice B. Toklas, but, generally, two women suggest gossip and a kiss goodbye. Kramer, still talking, meandered in a sea of non-existent purpose. I said, "Why are you talking about our purpose? Let's just say what we want to do."

I stopped him midmeander, then felt sorry, wishing I'd kept quiet, but he looked relieved—a little surprised, not offended. "Can you make a suggestion?"

I glanced at Cavanaugh. I was his guest and didn't want to embarrass him. I'd been too aggressive maybe; too impatient. He said, "Go on."

"I suggest each of us tell the story of his life."

The instant I said that I laughed, as if I'd intended a joke. What else could it be? I didn't tell the story of my life to strangers. Maybe I'd lived too long in California, or I'd given too many lectures at the university; or else I'd been influenced by Berliner, becoming a confessional person. Nobody else laughed. Cavanaugh looked at me with approval. Berliner grinned with rigid ferocity. He loved the suggestion. Kramer said, "I'll go first."

"You want to? You like the idea?"

"One of us can talk at each meeting. I have listened to numerous life stories in this room." Kramer, apparently, was a psychotherapist, but the room seemed an odd place for his business—all the plants, colors, art-work. It burst on every side with cries for attention, excitations, a maniacal fear of boredom.

"It will be good for me," he said, "to tell the story of my life, especially like this, in a nonprofessional context. It will be a challenge. I'm going to put it on tape. I will tape each of us."

I imagined him sitting among his plants and pot-tery listening to life stories, tape recorder going, dark face and tattoos presiding over all.

"Let's talk to one another, Kramer. No machines."

To my dismay Kramer yelled, "Why the hell not? I have so much talk on my tapes—friends, clients, lovers—that I don't even know what I have. So much I don't even remember."

I'd struck something sensitive, but I heard myself yelling back at him, a man who looked angry, even dangerous, "If you didn't put it on tape, you'd remember."

Everyone laughed, including Kramer. He said, "That's good, that's good." No anger at all. I was strangely pleased by this violence. I liked Kramer for laughing.

"That's very good. I'm going to write that down," he said.

"Yeah," said Cavanaugh, "no tape recorder. But

I want an idea of what this life-story business is like."

"You know what it's like," said Berliner. "It's like in the old movies when people were always talking to each other. Ingrid Bergman tells Humphrey Bogart about herself. Who she is. Where she's been. Then they screw."

A blond man wearing a pastel-blue sweater strained forward in his chair, saying, almost shouting, "I saw that movie. On the Late Show, right? Isn't that right?" He looked youthful and exceptionally clean. He wore cherry-red jogging shoes, creamy linen slacks, and clear-plastic-framed glasses.

All the faces became still. He retreated. "Maybe it was another movie."

Berliner's face swelled with astonishment, then tightened into eerie screeing, tortured noises: "Oh, man, what is your name?" He pointed at the blond. Kramer, hugging himself, contained his laughter. The blond said, "Harold," stiffening, recovering dignity. Tears like bits of glass formed in his eyes.

"Oh, Harold," said Berliner, "that's the story of my life. My mother used to say, 'Solly Berliner, why can't you be like Harold?' Harold Himmel was the smartest, nicest kid in Brooklyn."

"My name is Harold Canterbury."

"Right, man. Forgive me. A minute ago when you were talking, I had a weird thought. I thought—forgive me, man—you had a withered hand."

Harold raised his hands for everyone to see.

Kramer said, "Don't listen to that jackass, Harold. Nothing wrong with your hands. I'm getting more beer."

As he walked toward the kitchen, Cavanaugh followed, saying, "I don't know what this life-story business is about."

"I'll show you," said Kramer. "You get the beers."

Cavanaugh returned with the beers and Kramer with a metal footlocker, dragging it into our circle. A padlock knocked against the front. Kramer, squatting, tried to fit a key into the lock. His hands began shaking. Cavanaugh bent beside him. "You need a little help?" Kramer handed him the key, saying, "Do it." Cavanaugh inserted the key. The lock snapped open as if shocked by love.

Kramer heaved back the lid of the footlocker and withdrew to his pillow, lighting a cigarette, hands still shaking. "This is it, my life story." His voice labored against emotion. "You guys can see my junk, my trinkets. Photos, diaries, papers of every kind."

Had Kramer left the room it would have been easier to look, but he remained on his pillow staring at the open footlocker, his life. Paul suddenly scrambled toward it on hands and knees, looked, plucked out a handful of snapshots, and fanned them across the rug. Each of them bore an inscription. Paul read aloud: "Coney Island, 1953, Tina. Party at Josephine's, New Year's, 1965. Holiday Inn, New Orleans, 1975, Gwen." He looked from the photos to Kramer, smiling. "All these pictures in your box are women?"

Kramer, in the difficult voice, answered, "I have many photos. I have my navy discharge papers, my high-school diploma, my first driver's license. I have all my elementary-school notebooks, even spelling exams from the third grade. I have maybe twenty-five fountain pens. All my old passports. Everything is in that box."

Paul nodded, still smiling. "But these photos, Kramer. Are all these photos women?"

"I have had six hundred and twenty-two women."

"Right on," shouted Berliner, his soul projecting toward Kramer through big green eyes, doglike, waiting for a signal. Paul took out more photos and dropped them among the others. Over a hundred now, women in bathing suits, in winter coats, in fifties styles, sixties styles, seventies styles. Spirits of the decades. If men make history, women wear its look in their faces and figures. Fat during the Depression era; slender when times are good. But to me Kramer's women looked fundamentally the same. One poor sweetie between twenty and thirty years old forever. On a beach, leaning against a railing, a tree, a brick wall, with sun in her eyes, squinting at the camera. A hundred fragments, each complete if you cared to scrutinize. A whole person who could say her name. Maybe love Kramer. That she squinted touched me.

Kramer, with his meticulously sculpted hair, cigarette trembling in his fingers, waited. Nobody spoke, not even Berliner. Looking at the pictures, I was reminded of flashers. See this. It is my entire crotch.

Then Berliner blurted, "Great. Great. Let's do it. Let's all talk about our sexual experience." His face jerked in every direction, seeking encouragement.

As if he'd heard nothing, Kramer said, "I was born in Trenton, New Jersey. My father was a union organizer. In those days it was dangerous work. He was a communist, he lived for an idea. My mother believed in everything he said, but she was always depressed. She sat in the bedroom, in her robe, smoking cigarettes. She never cleaned the house. When I was six years old I was shopping and cooking, like my mother's mother. I cannot remember one minute which I can call my childhood. I was my mother's mother. I had a life with no beginning, no childhood."

"Right," said Berliner. "You had your childhood later. Six hundred and twenty-two mothers. Right?"

"The women are women. Eventually, I will have another six hundred. I don't know where my father is, but when I hear the word 'workers' or the word 'struggle,' I think of him. If I see a hardhat carrying a lunch pail, I think he is struggling. My mother now lives in New York. Twice a year I phone New York and get migraine headaches. Blindness. Nausea. Just say the area code 212 and I feel pain in my eyes."

I'd been looking at Kramer almost continuously, but now I noticed that his eyes didn't focus steadily. His right eye was slightly askew. He blinked and brought it into line with the other eye. After a while it drifted away again. He'd let it go for a moment, then blink, bringing it back. His voice was trancelike, compulsive, as if trying to tell us something before he was overwhelmed by doubt and confusion.

Cavanaugh said, "What about Nancy?"

"What about her?" Kramer sounded unsure who Nancy might be.

"Nancy Kramer. She lives here, doesn't she? These are her plants, aren't they?" Cavanaugh was looking at the photos on the rug, not the plants.

"You mean the women? What does Nancy think about my women?"

"That's right."

"We have a good understanding. Nancy goes out, too. It's cool. The plants are mine."

"Yours?" I said.

"Yes. I love them. I've got them on my tape recorder. I could play you the fig tree in the corner." Kramer said this with a sly, dopey look, trying to change the mood, trying to make a joke.

"Too much. Too much, Kramer," said Berliner. "My wife and me are exactly the same. I mean we also have an understanding."

I said, "Let Kramer talk."

Kramer shook his head and bent toward Berliner. "That's all right. Do you want to say more, Solly?"

Berliner looked at his knees like a guilty kid. "You go on. I'm sorry I interrupted."

Cavanaugh, imitating Kramer, bent toward Berliner. "Solly, aren't you jealous when your wife is making it with another guy?"

"Jealous?"

"Yeah, jealous."

"No, man. I'm liberated."

"What the hell does that mean?" I said.

Berliner said, as if it were obvious, "I don't feel anything."

"Liberated means you don't feel anything?"

"Yeah. I'm liberated."

Canterbury, with a huge stare of delight, began repeating, "You don't feel anything. You don't feel anything." Blond and lean, light blue eyes. He strained forward again to speak, then straightened quickly, as if he'd gone too far.

Berliner shrugged. "Once, I felt something."

Crossing and uncrossing his legs, seeming to writhe in his creamy slacks, Canterbury said, "Tell us about that, please. Tell us about the time you felt something."

"Does everyone want to hear?" said Berliner, looking at me.

I said, "Yes."

His voice flooded with accommodation. "We had a weekend in the mountains with another couple. A ski cabin near Lake Tahoe. The first night we got a little drunk after dinner and somebody—maybe me—yeah, yeah, me—I said let's trade partners. It was my own idea, right? So we traded. It was okay. It wasn't the first time we did it. But then I heard my wife moaning. It was a small cabin. And that was okay, but she was not just moaning. You know what I mean? She was moaning with love."

"Love?" said Kramer.

"Yeah. Moaning with love. She was overdoing it,

you know what I mean. She was doing love. I wanted to kill her."

Cavanaugh reached over and squeezed Berliner's arm. Berliner was still smiling, the green eyes searching our faces for the meaning of what he'd said. "Is that what you wanted to hear, Harold?"

"Did it ruin your weekend?"

"It was horrible, man. I lost my erection."

Berliner began screeing again and I heard myself doing it, too, like him, making that creepy sound.

"It was horrible, horrible. I was ashamed. I ran out of the cabin and sat on a rock. My wife started calling through the door, 'Solly, Solly, Solly Berliner.' Then she came outside, laughing, and found me. I showed her what she had done to me. She said it wasn't her fault. She said it was my idea. I hit her and said that was my idea, too. She started crying. Soon as she started crying, my erection came back."

Kramer said, "What happened next?"

"But you were talking, Kramer," I said. "You know what happened next. Next she hit him and they made it together. It's a cliché. You should finish telling your story. You should have a full turn."

Berliner, incoherent with excitement, shouted, "How the hell do you know? I'm telling what happened to me, me, me."

T H E   M E N ' S   C L U B

"All right, all right. What happened next?"

"She hit me and we made it together."

Cavanaugh, with two fists, hammered the rug until everyone quieted. Then he said, "Look at Kramer." Kramer was slumped forward, dark face hanging, glancing vaguely back at Cavanaugh.

"Let's let him alone," said Cavanaugh. Kramer grinned and sat up, but he didn't protest. Cavanaugh continued, "Maybe Kramer will want to say more later. I'd like to hear about the childhood he didn't have, but I think we're talking about love tonight. I'll tell you guys a love story. Okay?"

I said, "Kramer tells us he made it with six hundred women. Berliner says he traded his wife, then beat her up and had an erection. You call that love?"

Cavanaugh gave me a flat look, as if I'd become strange to him.

"Why not?"

"Oh, God."

"Hey, man, what do you want to hear about? Toothpaste and deodorants?"

"You're right, Cavanaugh. I give up. I bet your story is about how you made it with ten thousand high-school cheerleaders."

Cavanaugh stared at the place in the rug he had just

2 4

hammered. The big body was immobilized, the whole man getting things in order, remembering.

"About three months after we got married, my second wife and I started having arguments. Bad scenes. We would go to bed hating each other. There were months with no sex. I didn't know who was more miserable. I was making a lot of money playing ball and I was playing good. It should have been good for us altogether. The marriage should have been fine. In the middle of a game with the crowd screaming, I'd think this was no fantastic deal, because I had no love at home. Soon there was nothing in my body but anger. I got into fights with my own teammates. I couldn't shave without slicing my face. I was smoking cigarettes. I had something against my body and wanted to hurt it. When I told Sarah I was moving out, she said, 'Great.' She wanted to live alone. I moved out and stayed with a friend until I found an apartment. One day in the grocery store, I was throwing every kind of thing into my shopping cart. I was making sure nothing I needed would show up later as not being there. And this woman, I notice, is pushing her cart behind me, up and down the aisles, giggling. I knew she was giggling at me. When I got to the cashier she is behind me in line, still giggling, and then she says,

very sweet and tickled, 'You must have a station wagon
out there in the parking lot.' I said, 'I have a pickup
truck. Do you want a ride?' A man buying so much
food, she figured, has a family. Safe to ask for a ride.
She didn't have a car. I gave her a ride and carried
her groceries upstairs to her apartment. A little boy
was sitting on the floor watching TV. She introduced
us and offered me a drink and we sat in another room
talking. The boy took care of himself. Like in
Kramer's story. He cooked dinner for himself. He
gave himself a bath. Then went to bed. But his mother
wasn't depressed like Kramer's. She laughed and
teased me and asked a lot of questions. I talked about
myself for five or six hours. We ate dinner around
midnight, and then, at four in the morning, I woke
up in her bed, thinking about my ton of groceries
rotting in the pickup. But that wasn't what woke me.
What woke me was the feeling I wanted to go back
to my place. I hadn't left one woman to sleep with
another. I mean I hadn't left my wife to do that. I
wanted to go back to my own apartment, my own bed.
I didn't know what I was doing in this woman's bed.
I got up and dressed and left. As I was about to drive
away she comes running to the window of my pickup,
naked. 'Where are you going at this hour?' I said I
wanted to go home. She says, 'Okay, I'll come with

you.' I told her no and said I would phone her. She said okay and smiled and said good night. She was like that little boy. Or he was like her. Easy. Okay, okay, good night. I didn't think I would phone her. Now this is my story. I woke up the next afternoon. I liked it, waking alone, but I felt something strange. I wanted something. Then I remembered the woman and I knew what I wanted. I wanted to phone her. So I went to the phone and I realized I didn't know her number. I didn't even know her name. Well, I showered, got dressed, and stopped thinking about her. I went out for something. I didn't know what. I had everything I needed in the apartment. But I started driving and right away I was driving back to the grocery store, as if the pickup had a mind of its own. I was just holding the wheel. I didn't get farther than the grocery store, because I didn't remember where she lived. I remembered leaving the store with her, driving toward the bay, and that's all. She said, 'Turn right, turn left, go straight,' but I never noticed street names or anything. Now I wanted to see that woman more and more. The next day I went back to the grocery and hung around the parking lot. I did that every day for a week, at different times. I thought I remembered how she looked talking to me through the window of my pickup, how she smiled and said okay. I wanted to see her again badly. But I wasn't sure I could recognize her in the street. She was wearing gold loop earrings, jeans, and sandals. What if she came along in a skirt and heels? Anyhow, I never saw her again."

Cavanaugh stopped. It was obvious he had no more to say, but Kramer said, "Is that your story?"

"Yes." Cavanaugh leaned back, watching us.

"That's your love story?" I asked.

"Right. I fell in love with a woman I couldn't find the next day. She might live around the corner."

"You still love her?" asked Paul, tremendous delicacy in his voice, the slight small body poised, full of tenderness and tension.

Cavanaugh smiled at him with melancholy eyes. The whole expression of his great face and body suggested that he'd been humbled by fate.

"That can't be it," said Paul. "That can't be the end."

"The end."

"Cavanaugh," said Paul, "I've known you for years. How come you never told me that story?"

"Maybe I'm not sure it happened."

"You did go back to the grocery?"

"So what?"

I said, "Paul means, if you looked for her, it happened."

"I still look. When Sarah sends me out to do the shopping, she doesn't know the risk she's taking."

"Cavanaugh," I said, "do you think you ever passed her in the street and she recognized you but you didn't recognize her? That happened to me once. A woman stopped me and said, 'Hello,' and when I stood there staring like a fool, she turned and walked away. She'd recognized me."

"Anybody would recognize Cavanaugh," said Kramer, "from his picture in the papers."

"Hey," said Berliner, "I have an idea. We can all look for her. What do you say?"

Paul said, "Shut up, man."

"Why is everyone telling me to shut up? I drove here from San Jose and everyone tells me to shut up." Berliner sighed in a philosophical way. He'd seen into the nature of life. "Looking for Cavanaugh's woman. To me it's a good idea. Hey, man, I have a better idea. Cavanaugh, take a quick look through Kramer's snapshots."

"She wasn't one of them. She was a queen."

"Queen what?" shouted Kramer. "My women have names. What did you call her? You call her Queen?"

"I'm sorry, Kramer. Take it easy. He thinks I crapped on his harem."

I said, "Let me talk. I want to tell a love story."

"Great," said Berliner. "Everybody shut up. Go, man. Sing the blues."

"You don't want to hear my story? I listened to yours, Berliner."

"Yes he does," said Kramer. "Let him talk, Solly."

"I didn't try to stop him."

Cavanaugh said, "Just begin."

"Yeah," said Berliner, grinning, brilliant and stiff with teeth.

"So far," I said, "I've heard three stories about one thing. Cavanaugh calls it love. I call it stories about the other woman. By which I mean the one who is not the wife. To you guys, only the other woman is interesting. If there weren't first a wife, there couldn't be the other woman. Especially you, Berliner. Moaning, just moaning, your wife is only your wife. Moaning with love, she's the other woman. And Kramer with his snapshots. Look at them. He spent his life trying to photograph the other woman, but every time he snapped a picture it was like getting married. Like eliminating another woman from the possibility of being the other woman. And Cavanaugh, why can't he find his woman? Because if he finds her she won't be the other woman anymore. This way he protects his marriage. Every time he goes to the grocery store and doesn't see the other woman, which is every single time, his marriage is stronger."

Cavanaugh, frowning at me, said, "What are you trying to tell us? What's all this about the other woman? Why don't you say it, man?"

"I am saying it."

Kramer then said, "You're trying to tell us you love your wife. You think I don't love mine? You think Solly doesn't love his wife?"

Berliner cried, "If that's all you think, you're right. I hate my wife."

"Tell your story," said Cavanaugh. "Enough philosophy."

"I don't know if I can tell it. I never told it before. It's about a woman who was my friend in high school and college. Her name is Marilyn. We practically grew up together. She lives in Chicago now. She's a violinist in a symphony orchestra. I spent more time with her than any other woman except maybe my mother. She wasn't like a sister. She was like a friend, a very close friend. I couldn't have had such a friendship with a man. We'd go out together and if I brought her home late I'd stay over at her place, in the same bed.

Nothing sexual. Between us it would have been a
crime. We would fight plenty, say terrible things to
each other, but we were close. She phoned me every
day and we stayed on the phone for an hour. We went
to parties together when neither of us had a date.
Showing up with her increased my chances of meeting
some girl. It gave me a kind of power, walking in
with Marilyn, free to pick up somebody else. She had
the same power. We never analyzed our relationship,
but we joked about what other people thought. My
mother would answer the phone and if she heard
Marilyn's voice she'd say, 'It's your future wife.' But
she worried about us. She warned me that any woman
I was serious about would object to Marilyn. Or she'd
say it wasn't nice, me and Marilyn so thick with each
other, because I was ruining her chances of meeting a
man. That wasn't true. Marilyn had plenty of affairs.
All of them ended badly, but I had nothing to do with
that. One of her men scissored her dresses into rags.
Another flung her Siamese cat out the window. She
always found some guy who was well educated, had
pleasant manners, and turned out to be a brute. She
suffered, but nothing destroyed her. She had her vio-
lin. She also had me. Once, when I was out of a job
and no longer living at home with my mother, she
loaned me money and let me stay at her place for

weeks. I was trying to decide what to do—get another job, go back to school—and Marilyn didn't urge me to hurry. I didn't even have to ask her if I could stay at her place. I just appeared with my bags. One night she came home with a friend, a girl who looked something like her. Curly brown hair, blue eyes, and beautiful skin, faintly olive-colored. They were also the same size. Before dinner was over, Marilyn remembered something important she had to do. She excused herself and went to a movie. Her friend and I were alone in the apartment. It was glorious. A few days later, talking to Marilyn about this and that, I mentioned her friend. Marilyn said she didn't want to hear about her. That friendship was over and it was something she couldn't discuss. Furthermore, she said, I had acted badly that night at dinner, driving her out of her own apartment. I said, 'I thought you left as a favor to me. I thought you did it deliberately.' She said she did do it deliberately, but only because I made it extremely obvious that I wanted her to get out. Now I began to feel angry. I told her she didn't have to leave her own apartment for my sake and it was rotten of her to make me feel guilty about it after I'd started having very good feelings about her friend. I said this thinking it would prevent an argument; change everything. Marilyn would laugh; give me a hug. Instead, she lights a cigarette and begins smoking with quick half-drags, flicking ashes all over her couch. Then she says, 'Why don't you say that you consider me physically disgusting and you always have.' This was my old friend Marilyn speaking, but it seemed like science fiction. It looked like her. It sounded like her. It was her, but it wasn't. Some weird mongoose had seized her soul. Then she starts telling me about what is inside my head, things she has always known though I tried to hide them from her. Her voice is bitter and nasty. She says she knows I can't stand her breasts and the birthmark on her neck sickens me. I said, 'What birthmark?' She says, 'Who are you trying to kid? I've seen you looking at it a thousand times when you thought I didn't notice.' I sat down beside her on the couch. She says, 'Get away from me, you pig.' I felt confused. Ashamed and frightened at the same time. Then she jumps off the couch and strides out of the room. I hear her slamming around in the toilet, bottles toppling out of her medicine cabinet into the sink. Smashing. I said, 'Marilyn, are you all right?' No answer. Finally, she comes out wearing a bathrobe with nothing underneath and the robe is open. But she is standing there as if nothing has changed since she left the room, and she talks to me again in the same nasty voice. She sneers and ac-

cuses me of things I couldn't have imagined, let alone
thought about her, as she says I did, every day, all the
time, pretending I was her friend. Suddenly I'm full
of a new feeling. Not what a normal person would
call sexual feeling, but what does a penis know. It
isn't a connoisseur of normal sex. Besides, I was a lot
younger, still mystified by my own chemicals. I leap
off the couch and grab her. No, I find myself leaping,
grabbing her, and she's twisting, trying to hit me,
really fighting. She's seriously trying to hurt me, but
there's no screaming or cursing, there's only the two
of us breathing and sweating, and then she begins to
collapse, to slide toward the floor. Next thing I'm on
top of her. I'm wearing my clothes, she's lying on her
open robe. It's supernaturally exciting. Both of us are
shivering and wild. We fell asleep like that and we
slept at least an hour. I woke when I felt her moving.
The lights were on. We were looking at each other.
She says, 'This is very discouraging.' Then she went to
her bedroom and shut the door. I got up and followed
her and knocked at the door. She opens it and lets me
kiss her. Then she shut the door again. I went to sleep
in the living room, and left early the next morning. Six months later she wrote me a letter at my
mother's address, telling me about her new job in
Chicago and giving me her phone number. I phoned.

After we talked for a while, she asked about her friend. I told her it was finished between her friend and me. I was seeing somebody else. She changed the subject. Every few months I get a letter from her. I write to her also. Someday, if I happen to be in Chicago, I'll visit her."

In the silence following my story, I began to regret having told it. Then a man who had said nothing all evening asked, "Did you make it with Marilyn that night?"

"No. Nothing changed. I don't think it ever could."

The man started to say something, then stopped.

I said, "Do you have a question?"

It seemed he was a shy man. He said, "Was it a true story?"

"Yes."

He smiled. "I liked Marilyn."

"I like her, too. Maybe I can fix you up with her. What's your name?"

"I'm Terry."

"Terry?" shrieked Berliner. "Terry, you're supposed to phone your wife."

Grinning at Berliner, Terry seemed less a shy man than a man surprised. "It's not my wife," he said, intimating complexities. Old confusions. As if to forbid himself another word, he shook his head. Round and bald. Sandy tufts of hair beside the ears, like baby feathers. His eyes were hazel. His nose was a thick pull. "I mustn't bore you fellows with my situation." He nodded at me as if we had a special understanding. "We're enjoying ourselves, telling stories about love." He continued nodding. For no reason, I nodded back.

Cavanaugh said, "Talk about anything you like, Terry. You say the woman who phoned isn't your wife?"

He grinned. "I'm a haunted house. For me, yesterday is today. The woman who phoned is my former wife. A strange expression, but what else can I call her? Ex-wife?"

"Call her by her name," I said.

"Her name is Nicki."

"How long have you been divorced?" asked Cavanaugh.

"Usually one asks how long you've been married. Nicki and I have been divorced ten years. Nicki—"

"It's better," said Berliner, "if you say former wife. Nicki, Nicki—you sound like a ping-pong game."

"All right. After ten years of divorce we're closer than during our marriage. If you don't remarry, this is natural. She phones me two or three times a week. Listen to how personal I'm becoming. Why is everything personal so funny?"

"Who's laughing?" said Berliner. "Do you sleep together? To sleep with your former wife, I think—I mean just to me—I couldn't do it."

"You couldn't do it," I said. "Who asked you to?"

"He's right. I'm sorry, Terry."

"It doesn't happen often. Nicki has a boy friend. His name is Harrison. But they don't live together. Nicki can't get along with kids. She doesn't like kids. More complicated yet, Harrison's daughter, eleven years old, is a very sad fat girl. His boy, six years old, has learning problems. Harrison phones me, too. I meet him now and then to talk about his kids."

"He wants to talk to you?" I said.

"I'm a doctor. Even at parties people come up to me for an opinion. 'Terry, I shouldn't discuss professional matters in these circumstances, but my aged aunt Sophie has a wart on her buttock. She wants you to know.' "

"So what about Nicki? She was crying on the phone," Kramer says.

"She always does. Your Marilyn story reminded me of a fight we had when I was in medical school in Montreal. We lived in a two-room flat above a grocery store. It was a Saturday morning. I was studying at the kitchen table. Can I tell this story?"

Berliner said, "Only if it's miserable."

"A blizzard had been building for days. I watched it through the kitchen window as it attacked the city. The sky disappeared. The streets were dead. Nothing moved but wind and snow. In this deadly blizzard, Nicki decided to go out. She had been saving money for a particular pair of boots. Fine soft leather. Tight. Knee-high. They had a red-brown tone, like dried blood. Totally impractical and too elegant. The wind would tear them off her legs. Nobody in our crowd owned such boots. Our friends were like us—students. Poor. Always worried about money. Nicki had worked as a secretary all year. She never bought presents for herself. I had a tiny scholarship. It covered books and incidental tuition fees. We were badly in debt, but she wanted these boots. I don't know how she saved a penny for them. I pleaded with her not to go out in the blizzard. Something in my voice, maybe, suggested more anxiety about the price of the boots than her safety. The more I pleaded, the more determined she became."

"Why didn't you go with her?" I asked.

"I wanted to. But the idea of the boots—so trivial,

such a luxury—and her wanting to go get them that morning—made me furious. I could sympathize with her desire for beautiful boots. She deserved a reward. But why that minute? I was trying to study. My papers and books were on the kitchen table. Also a box of slides and a microscope I carried home from the laboratory. Today, though I own a house with ten rooms, I still use the kitchen table when I read medical journals or write an article. Anyhow, I was trying to study. I needed the time. It's difficult for me to memorize things, but I can do it if there is peace and quiet and no bad feelings in the air. You don't have to be a genius to be a doctor. But now I was furious. I yelled, 'Do what you like. Buy the stupid boots. Just leave me alone.' She slammed the door.

"For a while I sat with my papers and books. Outside the blizzard was hysterical. Inside it was warm and quiet. I worried about her, but my fury canceled the worry. Soon I began to study. I forgot about Nicki. Maybe three hours passed and, suddenly, she's home. Pale and burning and happy. I didn't say hello. My fury returned. She had a big shoe box under her arm. She had returned with her boots. While she put them on, I continued trying to study. I didn't watch her, but I could tell she needed help. The boots were tight. After a while she managed to get them on by herself, then she walked up to my table and stood there, waiting for me to notice. I could feel her excitement. She was trembling with pleasure. I knew what expression was in her face. Every muscle working not to smile. She waited for me to look up and admit she was magnificent in those boots. But the blizzard was in my heart. I refused to look. Suddenly my papers, books, slides, microscope—everything on the table was all over the kitchen floor. Nicki is strong. She plays tennis like a man. I felt I had been killed, wiped out of the world.

"She still claims I hit her. I don't remember. I remember rushing out into the blizzard with no coat or hat. Why? To buy a gun. I didn't really know what I wanted until I passed a pawnshop with guns in the window. I had a pocket watch that my father gave me when I left for medical school. Gold case. Gothic numerals. A classic watch. Also a heavy gold chain. In exchange for that watch I got a rifle. I asked the man for a bullet. I couldn't pay for it, but I told him the deal was off unless he gave me a bullet. He said, 'One bullet?' I screamed, 'Give me a bullet.' He gave it to me. If I'd asked for a ton of bullets, he would have thought nothing. Ask for one bullet and there's trouble."

"The police were waiting for you," said Berliner.

"The police car was in front of the house, its light blinking through the storm. I went around behind the house and climbed a stairway to the roof, and loaded the rifle. I intended to go to the flat and blow my brains out in front of Nicki."

"I thought you were going to shoot her," I said.

"Her? I'd never shoot her. I'm her slave. I wanted to make a point about our relationship. But the police were in the flat. I was on the roof with a loaded rifle, freezing in a storm. I aimed into the storm, toward the medical school, and fired. How could I shoot myself? I'd have been on that roof with a bullet in my head, covered by snow, and nobody would have found me until spring. What comes to mind when you commit suicide is amazing. Listen, I have a question. My story made me hungry. Is there anything to eat?"

Kramer rose from his pillow with a brooding face. "Men," he said, "Terry is hungry. I believe him because I too am hungry. I suppose all of us could use a little bite. I would suggest we send out for pizza. Or I myself would make us an omelet. But not tonight. You are lucky tonight. Very lucky. Tomorrow, in this room, Nancy is having a meeting of her women's group. So the refrigerator happens to be packed with good things. Let me itemize. In the refrigerator there is three different kinds of salad. There is big plates

of chicken, turkey, and salmon. There is also a pecan
pie. I love pecan pie. There is two pecan pies and
there is two lemon pies. There is a chocolate cake
which, even as I speak of it, sucks at me. I am offering
all this to you, men. Wait, Berliner. I have one more
thing to say, Berliner. In the alcove, behind the
kitchen, rests a case of zinfandel. It is good, good
California. Men, I offer to you this zinfandel."

Berliner was already in the kitchen. The rest of us
stayed to cheer Kramer. Even I cheered. Despite his
tattooed arms, which reminded me of snakes, I
cheered. His magnanimity was unqualified. No
smallest doubt or reluctance troubled his voice. Every
face in the room became like his, an animal touched
by glee. We were "lucky," said Kramer. Lucky,
maybe, to be men. Life is unfair business. Whoever
said otherwise? It is a billion bad shows, low blows,
and number one has more fun. The preparations for
the women's group would feed our club. The idea
of delicious food, taken this way, was thrilling. Had
it been there for us, it would have been pleasant. But
this was evil, like eating the other woman. We discovered Berliner on his knees before the refrigerator,
door open, his head inside. We cheered again, crowd-
ing up behind him as he passed things out to us, first
a long plate of salmon, the whole pink fish intact,

then the chicken, then a salad bowl sealed with a plastic sheet through which we saw dazzling green life. It would be a major feast, a huge eating. To Cavanaugh, standing beside me, I said, "I thought you had to leave early." He didn't reply. He pulled his watch off, slipped it into his pocket, and shouted, "I see pâté in there. I want that, too." The cheers came again. Some of the men had already started on the salmon, snatching pieces of it with their fingers. Kramer, who had gone to the alcove, reappeared with black bottles of zinfandel, two under his arms, two in his hands. He stopped, contemplated the scene in his kitchen, and his dark eyes glowed. His voice was all pleasure. "This is a wonderful club. This is a wonderful club."

Saint Augustine confesses to a night of vandalism with a gang of boys. They stole some pears. No big deal, but it troubled him that human company inspired evil. He hung out plenty. There was his mother, his mistress, his students, and always there were men. At Kramer's table with a gang who'd stolen more than pears, I felt no evil, only a kind of exhilaration, though I remembered telling my wife I'd be home early and I worried a little about that. Why? Because I had no urge to leave. Neither did anyone else. Even Canterbury, the lean blond man who told no stories and hardly ever laughed, was still here. I worried then for no reason, only for the sake of form, maybe, as when you're about to be unfaithful to your lover. How can I do this, you think, doing it. Paul and Berliner, to intensify the occasion, smoked marijuanas. The cigarettes quickened them grossly, putting nutty lights in their eyes. We'd eaten rapidly and very heavily, without much conversation, communicating in the action, in the food, deeper than words. Only Terry hadn't yet finished eating. He'd started on a second slice of pecan pie, chewing steadily and studiously, as if caught up in the sheer momentum of his personal meal. Paul and Berliner smoked. The rest of us drank wine, Kramer's good zinfandel. We'd emptied six bottles. Two more stood open on the table, beautiful things with long black necks and high curving shoulders. Watusi maidens.

Tomorrow, I supposed, my students would see me hung over, struggling with my voice. If one of them asked a question, I'd probably answer just the words and hope sense turned up on its own, like a lost dog. I didn't care about tomorrow. I was feeling adventurous, the way I used to feel years ago when I'd meet my buddies after school and say, "Let's shoot some eight ball." We'd take off for a pool hall in downtown Manhattan, morbid theater of men and sharp sensations. No natural light. No street sounds. You'd hear the gritty crunch and squeak as the tip of a cue is chalked, and the racks smacking slate, sliding across felt. Men always leaning against walls and smoking cigarettes or shuffling about the tables, "seeing," then calling, shots. I became one of them, cue stick gliding through the hook of my index finger toward a mottled bone-white moon ball. Then the measured stroke, soft thud, balls clacking, whirling apart, plopping into pockets. Always an ethical clock on the wall, but I didn't know about time as I leaned over luminous green felt in the shadowy dusty air. When I lost a game, a hot screw started to turn in my chest, a ferocious need to play another game, redeem my place among the men regardless of the time.

Later my mother would say, "You're ruining your life," thus reminding me of that enormous other thing to do. It came to me vaguely now, that other thing— classes to prepare, books to read. The kitchen faucet needed a new washer. There were cracks in the stucco walls of my house. The privet hedge out front was too tall, too bushy, millions of leaves striking in every direction, threatening property values with life. I would go home soon, put in a new washer, seal cracks, trim hedge, resume the homeowner's war against chaos. Right now I was at Kramer's table with the men.

Terry sat opposite me. Small muscles rippled in his

bald front. He chewed pecan pie, crushed the sticky
nuts to pulp. To my left, Berliner sat hunched, heavy
with deliberation, sipping his marijuana. Paul had
rolled the cigarette, then passed it to him with a con-
spiratorial wink. They were simpatico. Drug brothers.
To Paul's left sat Harold Canterbury—lean, pale,
static. He watched Paul twist a new paper around a
pile of desiccated grass. To Canterbury's left, at the
end of the table, big Cavanaugh. Bottle of wine before
him, neck enveloped in his hand. The sheen of eating
made his cheeks look swollen and metallic, his head
monumental, dominating silver, glass, ruined meats—
chicken, salmon, various pâtés—and marijuana smoke
winding above the devastation like an Oriental melody.
Slow, pythonic weight. How I felt, beneath my exhilaration, having eaten too much. My body was a philoso-
pher brooding on multitudes within as I gazed at a
salad bowl just beyond my plate. Green shreds clung
to the inner spin like leaves in a storm. Nobody spoke
for several minutes and then Berliner said, after
drawing marijuana essence into himself and savoring
fine effects, "Good grass." Paul nodded. These two,
beyond the rest of us, were feeling things. Berliner
nodded back at Paul, sealing their communion, his
white hair rising about his head like brain gas, so
startling I couldn't imagine how he sold anyone a

house. But of course the market was red-hot in California. A leper could sell a house. Kramer, at the end of the table opposite Cavanaugh, said, "Anyone care for coffee?" Nobody answered. There came only the sedulous crush of Terry's face, still eating. In the hazel eyes an eating look. Alert and blind. I stared at him in a particular way. Square shoulders. Round head. He had great physical integrity. When he ate, he ate, and he was made of fundamental shapes; peasant blood. Durable laborious strength lay beneath his mauve silk shirt. It complicated him with elegance, a feminine flow against his bulk. He moaned when he swallowed, as if his pleasure were so serious it could be expressed as pain. As the pie went down, his eyelids lowered. He appeared to swoon, to suffer deliciously. Beside his head the hand holding the fork looked small. Thick stunted thumb. Not a clever thumb, but strong-willed, capable of gouging, strangling. I remembered him telling us he was a doctor. Though he was only eating pie, I could have watched him for hours. Perhaps anyone thrown together with anyone else is community. I wondered if we ever really have to talk. Full of food, I was full of an approving spirit. We make discriminations; we marry a pretty face, good brains, a sense of humor. All such discriminations seemed vicious now. Terry, about to raise another piece of pie to his mouth, stopped. Looking at the pie, he said, "There was a woman who liked to taste my food in restaurants. Deborah Zeller. I went out with her for months. I almost married her, but something happened."

I could have said, "I was just thinking about marriage," but the coincidence was dull, a conversational dead end. I kept my mouth shut and waited. Terry looked for a response. He saw, in the bloated physiology of this hour, men too thick with sugars to want Deborah Zeller, a name of trills and thrusts. It hung in general density, then ceased when I heard the hum of a machine coming through the wall between dining room and kitchen. It was the refrigerator. Standing alone, raped, resonant with humiliation. Our ice mother. We'd seized her food.

A crime.

A crime for sure, but our very table—long pink heart of exotic wood—was also seized. A virtual tree ripped from the monkey jungles. Planed flat, sanded, oiled, rubbed until death yielded a mellow patina. The grain swirled like a river, forever moving and forever still. Aestheticized. As for our monkey kin, they stumbled on the ground. The jungle was gone. They were homeless, perishing; but the table was lovely and we were oblivious to any desperation. Brotherhood is exclusive, not universal. Freud says it's based on murder. He goes too far. Any dope can see, when beings unite, other beings die. A pride of lions is bad for zebras. A herd of zebras means less grass for cows. "Kramer," I said, "where did you get this table? I want one."

Kramer stirred in his darkness. Black hair, black eyes, tattooed forearms were turning toward me. "I want one," I said again, even as I lost interest in the thing.

"I bought it at Madera Shapes." He rubbed the surface like a sensitive skin and I felt as if I'd praised his child. "I use tung oil on it."

Berliner laughed. "You lick the table?"

"T-U-N-G. Tung oil. From a tree down South, from the nut."

"Oh," said Berliner, pinching the dregs of his marijuana, sucking it with sharply puckered lips. He took in the information about tung oil as he peered down the ridge of medial septum, his nostrils spreading, pulling with his eyes. Such difficulty and need. It suggested a woman's groin, distended, hauling her lover inside. I turned to Terry. "You say this woman, Deborah Zeller, tasted your food?"

Berliner collapsed, expelling smoke as if punctured.

"Graduate student in anthropology. Perhaps you knew her?"

"I knew a woman who liked to wear my clothes. She'd also sit on the edge of the tub and watch me shave. I watched her, too, but not the same way. I didn't want to be her."

"Oh, come on," said Berliner. "She put on your clothes and you put on hers. I like to wear my wife's panties." He laughed, coughing smoke. "It's natural. My wife once tried on my jock."

Paul said, "She must be fashion-conscious."

"Right, the whole thing is about getting naked." Berliner was thrilled by what he understood. The drug had mined his brain, delivering this truth to his mouth. He looked at us for acknowledgment.

Paul said, "Yeah." He sounded hopeful, willing to understand. "What whole thing, man?"

"The fashion industry. It's about getting naked." He waited for Paul, nodding at him, urging him to find this brilliance in himself.

"Yeah, yeah, but why do you think so?"

"When we have an argument," said Cavanaugh to nobody, "Sarah undresses in the bathroom."

"That so?" said Terry. "Nicki dressed when we had an argument. She'd put on makeup, fix her hair. I could be making a major statement about our marriage when I notice she is digging in the dresser for stockings. Next she is going out the door, car keys in her hand, as if she has a date. Then *varrrroom*, she's peeling rubber, taking off down the street."

Cavanaugh sighed. "I didn't mean Sarah undresses when we have an argument."

"No?"

"No. I mean I don't even know she's mad until she starts undressing in the bathroom, the door shut."

"I get it," said Terry, grinning.

"One time we were in the bedroom undressing. An argument started. She was naked by then. She grabbed up the blanket and top sheet, flung it around herself, and stood there yelling at me. I was so touched I started loving her, middle of her yelling. I couldn't hear the words. My dick was pointing at her like she'd been out of town for a month. I tried to concentrate on what she was saying. She said I made her feel like throwing up. Like I was my dick."

Cavanaugh laughed. Faces became sharp, wolfish, laughing with him, as if we'd seized an unexpected permission.

Berliner said, "The best place for being naked is New York."

"Yeah," said Paul, "I know what you mean." He was anxious to make up for his failure a moment ago. "So many people. You get naked just to know you exist. Right?"

"No, man. I mean the energy. You ever make it in Manhattan, around midtown?"

Paul snapped his fingers. "That's where it's at."

"You made it there?"

"No." He was smiling, shaking his head yes. "But it sounds right." He shrugged, his smile feeble, helpless. Smallest man in the room. Bird neck. Finicky fingers. Feelings came quickly to his face. It seemed fragile, easy to hurt. To rescue him, I said, "Berliner, when I get home I'll wake my wife and ask her to slip into my jock."

The green eyes released Paul, fixed on me, clicked toward a grim conclusion. Somewhere in his electricity he had my number. "You promise?"

I didn't know if I promised. I smiled at him. "Yes."

"You're an asshole. You want your wife to wear a jock."

He was smirking; triumphant. I wished he'd look at someone else. Kramer then said, "Terry, what about Deborah Zeller?"

"I'm ashamed." Terry was grinning. The word tickled him.

The word toppled Kramer into perplexity dark as himself. "This is the twentieth century," he said, glancing around the table, seeking consensus. "You shouldn't feel that way. In this club we tell everything. The whole point of being here."

"True, but I'm ashamed." He meant embarrassed, I supposed. He was being slightly coy.

"Have more wine," said Cavanaugh, noble face way up there, comprehensive as the sky. It seemed to mean: Look how I am. I talked about my wife and dick and I'm all right. Then he glanced down, studied his wineglass, rocking it, the stem pressed into the crotch of his thumb. He narrowed within himself; a hard, interior focus. Looking up at Berliner, then Paul, he said, "Every time you guys light a marijuana, I think you don't like your bodies. I always liked my body."

"Sure," said Berliner. "It made you a lot of money. I have an ulcer. You ever have trouble, Cavanaugh?"

"Yeah," said Paul. "My body has cost me a lot of money. I had asthma when I was a kid. I had a back operation. Wherever I travel, I get the local disease. Viruses meet me at the airport. I went to visit my sister in Kentucky and came home with chiggers. For days I was scratching my legs. My union had a conference in Hawaii. Like a paid vacation. I took my wife. First night in the hotel, I get bitten by a scorpion. I think there's about one scorpion in Hawaii. You ever have trouble like that, Cavanaugh? So I smoke a little grass. It rips off the top of my head. The less body the better, as far as I'm concerned."

Cavanaugh listened with a flat, unfriendly expression, as if he'd been taken by an access of bad will. It was hard to understand. I knew he'd drunk more than the rest of us, but he was huge and Irish; he could drink all night without poisoning his soul. Maybe he could be mean, but I'd never seen that in him, only the great athlete and gentle giant, the man who wanted his kids not to look like him.

He spoke to Paul now and it became clear that his expression had nothing to do with Paul or Berliner.

"I played ball for years. No tendonitis, no ruptures, no breaks, no sprains—and lately I have trouble with sleep. Put my head on the pillow and black out. I don't go to sleep. I faint."

Cavanaugh—superb in speed and strength, adored by millions—was sorry for himself. Paul and Berliner had missed the point. Their bodies gave them trouble, but they were normal.

"Who knows when he falls asleep?" said Berliner, surprised, but speaking softly; very solicitous. "If I'm falling asleep and I think, 'I'm falling asleep,' I wake up."

"Right, man. But for me the little trip, the nice couple of minutes between the pillow and nothing, is

gone. Middle of the night—same way I blacked out—
I wake up. I'm hungry. I have to go to the bathroom.
I want one of Sarah's cigarettes. I want to drink some
beers, get laid, look for a fight. This can be two in the
morning. I go stomping from room to room, slamming
doors, turning on lights. I'm mad. I want to go outside, shake the trees, wake the birds."

"I'll give you some Valium," said Kramer.

"I don't take pills. I'm a country boy. I get dressed
and drive to Oakland or San Francisco, or I head for
the San Rafael Bridge, pushing eighty, ninety. I'm
humming like a dynamo, faster than my pickup. I'm
going, going hot dog, and I don't know where I'm
going. Sometimes I drive to the park, leave the pickup
near the entrance, and run."

"Cold," I said.

"Yeah, cold," said Paul, close behind me.

"It's cold. Also dark. The trail is dim even in the
moonlight. But I've run it so much I could run it
blind. Deer standing in the meadows don't look at me
anymore. I once passed a doe who was defecating and
she went right on, not even twitching an ear. As if I
was irrelevant. I run so long sometimes I see colors
begin, hear birds chirping in the fog."

I looked beyond Cavanaugh to the dining-room
wall. Red velvety paper, a bloody sheen giving pres-

sure to the whole room, walls closing in, pulsing. Too sensational. Not a room in which to try to think, but I wanted to say something. "What do you do then?"

Paul muttered the same question. It seemed we asked.

"I shower and dress for work. Slowly. I feel confused. I worry. Which tie to wear? Which shirt? Once I came back, my body screaming like it was permanently awake. I took a long shower and got back into bed. I had to be able to sleep. I'd run fifteen miles. Nothing happened. Sarah was curled up like a fist around an egg. Hot with sleep, gone away, sleeping with sleep. Not me. I had nothing. I wasn't consistent with my body."

"Oh, man," said Berliner, as if he couldn't bear another word. "You should have balled her. When I can't sleep, I ball Sheila and konk right out."

"I started touching her. Just for company. I slid my hand along her leg and, after a while, I wanted more. I pulled her under me. She was asleep. I had an idea I could do it without waking her. I had her all arranged and was fixing to do it. She said, 'Aw, Cavanaugh, for Christ's sake. Later.' She wasn't really awake, but I felt put down worse than if she had been. Bitter. I felt cheated, denied my natural right to sleep. I thought, Sarah and I are married to one another. In so many words: 'Sarah and I are married to one another.' "

"Each other," I said, unbalanced, unable to stop myself.

"That's what I meant. I thought how come we aren't one flesh? You are one. I am one. I said she was a conventional bitch, not wanting to fuck me at 5 a.m. Always later. 'Later' means after dinner. The meal half-digested. Dishwasher chugging in the kitchen. 'Later' means the neighbor's TV blasting in your window. One of my kids coughing in his room. You know what it's like trying to fuck when your kid is coughing? I said she wanted to bring me down, make me do it on schedule like every married asshole in America. I was making a speech in the dark. She was curled up, her back to me. Her position. She'd gone right into it while I was talking. All of a sudden the bed dips and she's lunging out of it, standing over me, crying. She said, 'You're doing this to torture me. Why are you torturing me? Night after night.' I pulled her down. She didn't resist. She would have let me, but I didn't ball her. She wouldn't have gotten up for the kids later. I'd have had to make their breakfast and pack their lunches."

Cavanaugh stopped. Berliner said, "Yeah," as if relieved. The word carried other colors, too—consent,

condolence, amen—like a small, squalid bouquet.
Paul echoed Berliner. "Yeah."

Yeah-yeah was better than silence, but I wanted to
add something. It was time to be supportive, as they
say. Go out of oneself feelingly. Leap the psychic
fence. Stand in Cavanaugh's space. Let him know I
feel what he feels. Properties of the heart are taxed
by friendship. But I was tight. I felt implicated in
Cavanaugh's marital agonies. I'd merely listened to
him and now I felt implicated. I couldn't say that. It
sounded moral.

Kramer said the point of the club was to tell everything. Should Cavanaugh have told me about Sarah?
She was my friend. I didn't want to know what she
didn't know I knew about her. I remembered Cavanaugh with other women, especially at college parties
years ago. He always left with the prettiest ones. They
looked virginal and obedient beside him, going off
into the sexual night. How awesome. Like a religious
experience. Cavanaugh was so huge. A famous athlete
with the handsome, arrogant head of a warrior. Steep
cliff-like cheeks and bright small eyes, tilted, high in
his face. I'd seen that structure—long vertical planes
and slanted eye slits—hammered into the steel of
ancient helmets. He descended from heroes. Invincible, murderous, rapacious stock. Sarah wouldn't fuck

him at 5 a.m. What had the world come to? But why should she be so accommodating? Did his lunatic hard-on even have her particularly in mind? He'd begun to change; the great body was being taken from him, alienated by weird sleep rhythms. After midnight he springs from bed. He wants to fight, drink, speed, fuck. I thought of him driving the San Rafael Bridge in his pickup, ninety miles an hour, Angel Island looming in the black and moonlit bay, then the walls of San Quentin and the hills beyond. I could feel the undulations of the long bridge. My brain, trying to think what to say, wandered in images. Berliner mumbled, "Yeah," as if Cavanaugh's trouble, like a boulder, rumbled down his soul. Then he said, "Sex and sleep." Words falling like pieces of life, dull, without relation, from disparate realms. Something came to me.

The great complaint of women: "You turn over after sex and go to sleep." Then a sex-and-sleep story told to me by a student, Gilda Jordan, undergraduate from Malibu. Twenty years old, but with the brittle sophistication of a much older person. Tough laugh. Quick mouth. A scar like a silver hair beside her right eye. When she talked her hands were flags, agitating her bracelets, slapping at her necklace. The scar was another adornment, part of her activity, clatter, quickness. She called me by my first name. During office hours she'd stick her head in the doorway. "When is the final paper due?" She'd laugh. For her, the question was absurd, unreal, as if she were a "student." Her father produced movies; she'd grown up with a movie mentality. Whatever she was, she "was." Except for her scar. If she sat still for a moment, it would begin quietly to insist it was a scar. I'd wave her inside. She'd take the chair beside my desk, lighting a cigarette, and all at once start to gossip about herself.

The sex-and-sleep story came with a lot of laughs. She'd met this guy, laugh, and he inserted his penis into her. Laugh. "I mean we went to bed first." She leaned toward me, slapped my knee, laughing. "You hear what I said?" Anyhow, he lay there, inside her, laugh, not moving even a little bit, laugh, laugh, laugh. Minutes passed. Then he twitched. He came. "Didn't feel licit," she cried, laugh, oh laugh. She had to drag herself out from under him because he was asleep. She felt she'd been fucked by an insect. She laughed. I laughed. Sex wakes women—think of Sleeping Beauty—and puts men to sleep.

In the belly of my wineglass looped a ruby pool of zinfandel. Dumb good substance. Unlike Cavanaugh running after annihilation. I had nothing to say. He felt unknown. Irrelevant. Deer didn't look at him. I didn't either. I looked beyond his head when I glanced in his direction. I saw the wallpaper and a dish cabinet standing beside the kitchen door. Old yellow pine. Brown knots like birthmarks and a tall glass front. Deep shelves stacked with china and knickknacks, tiny pink pigs and dancing yokels. Porcelain sillies. It didn't suit decent old pine. Neither did the wallpaper. In Kramer's house nothing suited anything and all of it seemed chosen.

A house of blatant heart, yearnings for excitement, everywhere in different styles. Orange rug in the living room. Glossy acrylics on the walls. The opposite of puritanical is the savage energy of bad taste. Cavanaugh was pouring himself more wine. He said, "Come on, Terry. Your turn."

"Yeah," said Berliner, "tell us about Deborah Zeller."

"Graduate student," I said. Terry looked confused, as if he were waiting for us to tell him his story. "You said you almost married her, then you stopped talking."

"Don't be ashamed," said Cavanaugh. "Don't feel crap like that. Kramer's right, man. This is the twentieth century. We didn't come here tonight to feel ashamed."

Canterbury said, "Oh, let him alone." But he'd been quiet so long he'd lost the power of being heard. A psychological superfluity at this table, in this house. Lean ghostly fellow wearing glasses and pastels.

Terry said, "I believe I see your point, Cavanaugh. Shame is old-fashioned. I'll write a paper on the subject for a medical journal. What should I feel in the meantime?"

"Feel guilt," I said. "Tell what happened with Deborah Zeller. Don't leave anything out." I spoke as if to meet his irony, but I was thinking still of Cavanaugh. Though we'd been friends for years, he never talked of very personal matters. A sociologist says a woman appears half-naked at a party, but, with one man, she'd never dress that way. The principle applied here. In a crowd Cavanaugh could say anything.

Canterbury sneered at me, the expression fleeting, minimal, difficult to interpret. I wasn't even sure I'd seen it. Had I offended him by urging Terry to talk? He was looking at me. I looked back, as if seeing him for the first time. Pale and blond. Lunar qualities. White negative space, like conscience. He said nothing. I looked down.

"It's very silly," said Terry. "Shortly after my divorce I met a woman named Deborah Zeller—"

"Wait," cried Berliner, rising. "Shortly after my divorce I met a woman." He was striding away, passing through the living room, heading for the stairs, running up, shouting, "Don't say another word until I piss."

Terry lowered his voice. "I married young. I didn't know much about women."

"I hear you," shouted Berliner.

"Amazing," said Terry. He waited. Everyone waited, including Deborah Zeller, the name so familiar it felt like a thing. Chunky. Bulging. Almost hot. My mother used to say, when I sneezed, "Somebody is talking about you." I imagined Deborah Zeller sneezing, and, upstairs near the roof, Berliner. He stood with legs spread, like a statue at the bowl. The trousers of his gray polyester suit were open. He held his dick. Green eyes watched the urine plunge. He pissed long and long.

THREE

"I wait like an ox," says Kafka. Masochists don't mind waiting, but most people do. It's a miserable, degrading thing, a social torture inflicted on convicts and dogs. I wondered if Berliner had a problem pissing. He'd said his body gave him trouble. He'd also said, "Don't say another word," and here we were, six male heads around a table, waiting in silence.

In the middle of the table lay a salmon head, like an emblem of our situation. Not so different from our heads—intact, open-eyed, stopped—except for the slick sheath of skin, trailing spine, murdered mouth. It looked as if it had been devoured in flight, so quickly devoured it was unaware that it was dead. A waiting look. Thus, I identified waiting and death. "My wife told me a waiting story," I said, determined to disobey Berliner; to talk and not to feel dead.

Terry put down his fork and looked at me as if this subject—waiting—engaged him crucially. Perhaps it did. Doctors have waiting rooms. His attention, like his great bald head, made an impression of solidity and fullness. I didn't feel equal to it, but I proceeded mechanically to talk.

"The story is about when she was a little girl and lived with her mother."

"Yes," said Terry.

"Her parents were divorced. Her mother worked."

"Yes," he said. The word pressed me like a finger. I picked up speed.

"She used to walk home from school alone. When she got to the apartment and put the key in the lock, she'd feel frightened. Her mother worked late. The apartment was always empty in the afternoon, but she imagined someone was inside, waiting for her. She'd open the door, hurry straight to the TV set, and sit down in front of it on the rug. She remained there until her mother came home. She wouldn't move, wouldn't even take off her coat and gloves. One afternoon, sitting close to the TV set, she had to wait longer than usual. It got dark. She flicked on the TV. A face

appeared. It held her. A man in a white suit. He was
talking to her. His voice was full of love. It was like
'a deep silver spoon,' she says. He was exhorting her
to believe, telling her it was good to believe, and he
kept on smiling as he talked, showing her how good
it was. Alone in the dark apartment with this man
talking to her, she heard herself begin whimpering,
'I believe, I believe.' "

Terry smiled, then said, "I don't get it."

I felt a rush of embarrassment, as if I'd told a joke
badly. Now, glancing at the salmon head, it was nothing but the head of a dead fish. "Doesn't matter," I
said. "I don't get it either. I could tell other stories that
have no point. This often happens to me. I start to
talk, thinking there is a point, and then it never arrives.
What is it, anyhow, this point? Things happen. You
remember. That's all. If you take a large perspective,
you'll realize there never is a point. There's only a
perspective. For example, look at that salmon head.
The poor dumb fish was swimming upstream and his
head landed in that plate."

"But I get it," said Paul, turning an intimate face
to me. "I see what you mean. I have an old friend
named Mitch. He was always late. I was always waiting. Skinny guy with glasses and crooked teeth. He
could give you a look, you'd crack up laughing. I

loved him. Everybody loved him. Five years ago he phoned. I hadn't heard his voice in a long time, but right away I said, 'Mitch, Mitch. It's you, for God's sake.' You know what he said? He said, 'Who is this?' " Paul stopped and shook his head. To settle his feelings. Make them collect.

"He'd phoned me by accident. He was in Memphis and couldn't stay on the line. Too expensive. I told him to hang up, let me call him. When I called, it was the wrong number. I was so frustrated I kicked the wall. Then I calmed down. I sat by the phone, staring at it, waiting, smoking cigarettes, praying it would ring. It didn't ring. Then, last week—five years later —the phone rings and it's Mitch. He says he's in Berkeley. I recognized his voice right away and this was no mistake. He phoned me. He wanted to talk to me. I almost went crazy with happiness. He came by to my place, the same funny Mitch with the glasses, the crooked teeth. I asked if he remembered the time I loaned him fifty bucks. Years ago in New York. I had to get fifty bucks and meet him on a corner uptown, near the park. He sounded desperate. I ran to the bank. There was forty-two bucks in my account. I wrote a check for fifty. I was scared. Man, if some guard pulled his gun on me, I would have thought it was natural. But the bank was busy. Long lines. They

cashed my check without looking. I asked Mitch if
he remembered how cold it was, how it was snowing.
He laughed. I could see he remembered. But talk
about waiting. Man, I waited in the cold, fifty bucks
balled up in my fist. Three hours late, Mitch arrives
in a taxi. I couldn't believe it. He shows up three hours
late in a taxi with a dynamite black chick sitting beside him. He took the fifty bucks through the window.
I didn't even have change for the subway. I walked
home. 'I still owe you that fifty,' he says. I told him
forget it. Seeing him was worth more than fifty bucks.
Then he says his luggage was lost at the airport and
he has a big appointment in San Francisco. Could I
lend him a tie and a nice pair of shoes? I found him
a tie. The shoes were beautiful, handmade in London.
A little tight, but they looked great. I'd worn them
only once. Mitch said he could have them stretched.
He knew a 'cobbler' in San Francisco, retired army
officer who'd had an eye shot out in the Africa
campaign. We laughed. Mitch always knows somebody. Whatever you want, he knows somebody.
Drop Mitch anyplace in America, even in the world,
he'll have connections. He'll know a guy who can fix
your watch. Another guy who can do a first-class
valve job, cheap. Another guy who can get you some
coke. A woman whose sister's boy friend can get you

a machine gun. He knows a chiropractor who does abortions for twenty-five bucks. Mitch said he couldn't hang around. He'd come back after his appointment. We could talk then. He wanted to hear how I'd been doing. He wanted to meet my wife and kids. He had things to tell me about himself. I was so excited I didn't go to bed. What if I fell asleep and didn't hear the doorbell? My wife woke me at four in the morning. I was asleep in the kitchen, my head on the table. She said, 'Mitch isn't coming.' She pulled me upstairs to bed."

Terry said, "I must be slow tonight. I don't seem to understand things. You say, after five years he shows up, takes your tie and shoes, and he disappears."

"It's just shoes. Just shoes. A tie. It's clothes, you dig?"

"If you hit him in the face, I would dig."

"You should see his face. Long skinny face with snaggle teeth. He looks like a broken stork. When they cashed my check, the money was for Mitch. If it was for me, the guard would have blown my head off. Everybody loves Mitch. The bank didn't know the money was for him, but if it was for me they would have looked at my account. They would have said, 'Only forty-two bucks in your account, mister. Get your ass out of here.' You think I could hit him in the face? Man, I was walking home broke after waiting three hours in the cold to give him fifty bucks, and I didn't even feel angry. I couldn't hit Mitch."

"I hear you," shouted Berliner, his footsteps coming downstairs, turning into the hall to the kitchen. Paul grinned and shut up. Through the kitchen wall, Berliner said, "Shortly after my divorce, I screwed Deborah Zeller."

Poor Deborah Zeller, I thought, compared to Mitch.

The kitchen's swinging door jolted, shoved wide. Berliner stood in it, reborn. "Go on, baby. You were saying 'shortly.' I like that word. I'm going to use it, too, shortly."

Cavanaugh said, "Sit down, man, or I'll kill you."

Paul was still grinning, delighted by Berliner's return. His grin made him look sort of stupid, but he was merely loyal. He'd die for a buddy.

Deborah Zeller."

too, shortly."

FOUR

Not sitting, Berliner said, "I've been thinking about your sleep trouble." He leered at Cavanaugh, the expression magnifying his features, freeing light in his eyes, making long, evil teeth. "A marriage bed has benefits. You fart in it and nobody is offended."

Cavanaugh's voice was weary and severe as he said, "A marriage bed has benefits. I appreciate what you're saying. When I do it with another woman I have to wash afterwards."

Berliner sat. Again triumphant. White hairs coiled in his nostrils, like incandescent wires, seething.

"What are you talking about, Cavanaugh?" I asked the question exactly as if I didn't know what he was talking about. My face was hot.

"I wash and check my clothes for hairs. I chew gum, worry about sex stinks, marks on my body. You know. Not worth it, man. The time. The phony conversation. I hate the kissing in particular. It makes me think of Sarah. How many ways can you kiss a woman? Then having to be charming for two or three hours in the afternoon. I drive home thinking I'll never do this again. But I do it again."

"You do?"

"Yeah. I do things I don't like to think of myself doing. I don't like being the kind of man who likes doing it. Except I like it. Man, what am I talking about?"

"Making it with another woman," said Kramer. "You lie to Sarah?"

"I talk with half my head. The other half doesn't exist. I don't lie to her, I lie to myself. I come home after doing it. I can't get there fast enough. Dinner is ready, table is set, kids are cleaned up and waiting for me. A jar of daisies is in the center of the table. Milk is set out for the kids. Like nothing happened. This is it, the way it is and it should be. White, yellow, clean. Even the cat looks happy. I lift the fork to my mouth and catch a whiff of cunt, because twenty minutes ago I was fucking my brains out down the road. I scrubbed good, but there it is. The kids are laughing. They knock over a glass of milk. Sarah says to me, 'You have to make them behave. I can't be the only one who does that.' I yell, 'Behave, or I'll rip your heads off.' They giggle and Sarah wants to kill me. I tell her to get the daisies off the table. They take up too much room. We don't need daisies when we're trying to eat dinner. Man, I like those daisies and I'm telling her to get rid of them."

Kramer grinned.

Cavanaugh grinned back at him. "That's not how it is for you?"

"No."

"No kids. For you, bullshit is a way of life. How come you never turned gay?"

"I've got bleeding piles. Don't get personal, Cavanaugh."

"My wife is pretty," I said, a maudlin slide in my voice.

"So?" Cavanaugh glanced at me with irritation.

"She moves pretty. She sits cross-legged in the middle of the quilt and brushes her hair. I see her do this every night. Her head tips against the stroke and I hear a fiery rush as the brush goes down. She finishes. Removes her glasses. She sticks them into one of her slippers, then goes to sleep."

"So?"

"If I made it with another woman, it would degrade my wife."

"If she didn't know?"

"She'd get sick."

"Right," said Paul. "Right, right. She'd get very sick. She'd need an operation. The doctors would cut out her machinery. You like the way she brushes her hair?"

"I depend on it."

"My wife does yoga before she goes to bed," said Paul, looking at his reflection in me. "That's eloquent, man. The way she brushes her hair."

"Hey," said Berliner, sitting up sharply, staring toward the horizon of his mind. "Every night I see this dog. Legs like pins. Every night. Old Japanese man comes down the street, the dog bouncing in front of him, sniffing bushes, cutting his eyes back to see if the man is coming. It goes bouncing out onto the asphalt. Tiny dog. Nails like rats scratching the asphalt. The man stays at the curb and the dog makes circles, tiny scratchy steps. Million to the inch, tighter and tighter circles, sniffing, trembling. The man lights a cigarette to show the dog he is being patient. The dog keeps circling, looking for the exact spot. Toothpick tail sticks up straight. He is about to squat and crap. But he has to do one more circle, then one more, then one more. He never craps."

"No?" said Paul, his voice all charity. "How come?"

"It isn't in his nature anymore. He does the circles for the man."

"What are you talking about?" asked Cavanaugh.

"Freedom, baby. I'm talking about freedom." Berliner's eyes were big with vision, with desire to share it. Cavanaugh delivered us. He said, "I see what you're getting at, Solly. But I'm not a little dog. I'm a pinball machine. One woman makes another necessary. I used to show up at parties with Miss Beautiful and I'd be looking at every other woman in the room. I'd feel trapped for the evening. You know what I used to do on the road?"

"What?" I said.

"I told Sarah about it."

"What did you do on the road?"

"I told her I was sorry. It was our anniversary. The kids were staying with my mother. We went camping up north. High pine woods. River. Burning yellow moon. Suddenly I had to tell her everything and I felt it would be okay. I told her about Kansas

City, El Paso, New York—the women. You wouldn't
believe what she said. She said, 'I want a divorce.' I
told her it wouldn't happen again. I wanted her to
forgive me. She said, 'I want a divorce.' Like I had
one in my pocket. I was getting irritated. I promised
her it would never happen again. She says she wants
a fucking divorce. Then she says, 'Okay. Me or
basketball.' "

"You picked her," said Paul.

"Damn right."

Paul grinned, looking very pleased.

"And it still happens," said Cavanaugh, "every
chance I get. But I don't move on the wives of friends.
Never. I absolutely draw the line there. Except sometimes."

"You lack inner resources," said Terry. "It's not
serious."

"I love to fuck. That's serious. It's going to be my
epitaph. Cavanaugh loved to fuck."

Terry lifted a piece of pie to his lips and said,
"Personally, I prefer courtship." The pie slipped
into his mouth. He chewed. I looked at his stunted
thumbs. Brutal digits. He preferred courtship. Things
figure in the human world to the degree they don't.

"What did you do on the road, Cavanaugh?" I
asked the question, unsure he hadn't actually told us.

"A lot of courtship."

Except for me and Canterbury, everyone laughed. Berliner, eyes still bearing diffuse visionary luster, said, "I spent a little time on the road, but I'm not Cavanaugh. I never did courtship. I never showed up at a party with a beautiful woman. If I had one I wouldn't take her to a party."

Cavanaugh grinned, started to laugh, stopped. Berliner's eyes had become sorrowful, more wretched than mystical. Whatever he looked at, he didn't want to see.

"I can dig it," said Paul. Berliner continued as if there had been no gap in his talk.

"But like I met this woman in Baton Rouge, in a motel parking lot, leaning against a green Cadillac the color of poison. Drunk. She was so drunk. I parked my car and was walking by, trying not to notice. She says, 'Bud, you do it good. I been watching you. Help me park my car.'"

He mimicked the woman's accent, new tones in his voice; gentle, very gentle. I was surprised, touched, slightly ashamed of myself. Berliner had acting talent. It wasn't that the woman lived, but that I could feel how she lived for him. I'd misjudged Berliner. The crazy spasmodic had feelings.

"She scratched up the side of her Cadillac trying to get it between two other cars. She was too drunk to do it right. So she quit, left the Cadillac sticking out in the aisle, at an angle. She was leaning against the door, tangled up in herself. She had a cigarette in her mouth and there were butts dumped all around her feet. She'd emptied the ashtray, like to mess up the world so it would be no different from herself. I smelled ugly perfume. She gives me the keys and I climb into her Cadillac. Inside, it was like her outside, stinking perfume. A lot of burns in the seat leather. I see powder jars, hairpins, a hairbrush. Maybe a hundred balls of tissue paper on the seat and all over the floor. I started the car, backed out, then pulled it in straight. When I got out and handed her the keys, I say, just to say something, 'I also have trouble parking. It's one of the miseries of my life.' She says, 'We got nothing in common, bud. Don't put the moves on me.' I hear don't, I think do, but this is the thing. I'm standing close, staring at her. I see that even if she wasn't a mess, she isn't perfect. Okay. But like she has long eyes with points, like leaves. Silver pupils looking up at me through her hair. Red stuff from a knifed couch, like. She isn't perfect, you know what I mean, but she's got these eyes. Better than perfect. I mean, I was thinking this repulsive

broad is really beautiful. Even drunk, she is cutting
me up with her eyes. I feel myself starting to shake.
I'm scared. Like a stupid kid. I don't know what to do.
I been around, but I don't know what to do. So I put
out my arm. She tells me to fuck off and I want to die.
I'm humiliated. Why? Is she going to tell anyone
Solly Berliner tried to pick her up? Who cares? I
didn't know anybody in that town. I could walk away
and never see her again. But I stand there, dying, my
arm sticking out. She falls on it. She didn't take it,
she falls on it. To me it was the same. I'm now dragging her around the parking lot, holding her up, and
she's flopping along beside me. Then she vomits. All
over my fucking shoes. It was disgusting, but I didn't
complain. I walked her into the motel bar and ordered some coffee. I went to the men's room, cleaned
my shoes. When I came out I ordered a drink for
myself and sat with her. A jazz band was playing.
Bass, sax, drums, piano. Real good. It was nice. Like
we were having a date. She drank her coffee and
talked. I made listening noises, that's all. I was hoping she would sober up, but not too quick. I asked if
she wanted more coffee so she wouldn't think I'm an
animal. You know what I mean? She says no, then
says she feels awful about what she did to my shoes.
I laughed it off, then called for the check. Cool. In

control. I stood up and held out my arm. She gets up
and comes with me. We go out of the bar, then down
the hall toward my room and she doesn't say anything.
At the door, when I'm putting in the key, she says,
'Don't try anything with me, bud.' Maybe a minute and
a half later, we're on the bed. She didn't have all her
clothes off. I couldn't believe it. She was holding me
and kissing me like I was her teddy bear. I was still
wearing my shirt and socks. Next morning her eyes
are waiting for me. Sober. In her sleep something
piled up behind them. Like bad smoke. I figured she
was studying her big mistake. Me. Maybe hating herself, wanting me to get out so she could shower, wash
it away. I don't look too good first thing in the morning. I couldn't blame her for having like regrets. But
that wasn't my problem. She came to my room. She
says, looking at me, 'You're a nice chap.' I went to
the toilet. I had no feeling. Not any. The sun was
shining. I had a plane to catch. My business in town,
buying into this property for a corporation, was finished. A waste of time. These Southern bastards never
planned to let me in. They made me fly down to shit
on me. She lay there watching me dress. I didn't bother
to shave. I don't think I said one word. I was at the
door, bags in my hands, when I feel her. She's press-
ing against my back, her hands on my shoulders.

She says, 'How am I to write you a letter? I don't even know your zip code.' I put down my bags and turned. I was going to say something, but she kissed me and put her tongue in my mouth. It was like she liked me. I started to kiss her, too, the same way. I think she really liked me. You know what I mean? I started thinking I would cancel my reservation, make another one. I could still phone Sheila, tell her not to meet me at the airport. I could tell her I'd be a couple of days late. I think she liked me a lot. But I had to go. I had my ticket. I got to the airport just in time to turn in the rented car and catch the plane. Sheila was waiting to drive me back to town. I said I had to talk to her. She says, 'Talk.' I said, 'When we get home.' She was curious, but like impatient. All the way home I was planning what to say. When we got home she says, 'Okay, talk. You made the deal?' I told her to sit down. Listen. She sits. I started to say something, I don't even know what, but then I couldn't. I lay down on the floor with my bags. She is looking at me, wondering was I going to play a stupid joke. I said, 'Come down here.' She dropped down on her knees. Not like she wanted to. She says, 'Okay, what? You buy into the property? What?' I said, 'Kiss me. Put your tongue in my mouth.' She says, 'I thought you had to talk.' I said, 'Put your tongue in my mouth.'

She looks at me a long time, then says, 'I will not.' I wanted to punch her right in the head, but I only lay there feeling sorry for myself. For her, too, you know. I understood the whole problem of our marriage. Sheila doesn't like me."

Cavanaugh said, "Solly, did you tell that story for me?"

Berliner shrugged. "It just came out."

Paul reached a fresh marijuana toward him. Berliner glanced at the cigarette as if he didn't know what it was.

"That's for telling your story, man."

Berliner took the cigarette and lit it, pulling gas uphill in stages.

"You didn't know your wife didn't like you?" said Terry.

"A marriage. A marriage. You know, man. Any little thing makes you angry. I go to the grocery and forget to buy coffee. Sheila says there must be something fundamentally wrong with my brain. She looks like she wishes I was dead. Because of the coffee. I laugh. But I didn't know the worst until I met the woman in Baton Rouge."

"She put her tongue in your mouth. That's how you knew?"

"It was words. How come I didn't have the words until then? Once I took a class in night school. Great Ideas of the West. I bought a special notebook to write down what the professor said. But I didn't write anything. He was always saying, like, 'How do I know this table exists?' A fucking table. That's no problem. It's so boring it has to exist. The problem isn't tables, you dig? I got stupid sitting in that class, paying money to hear a shmuck talk about tables."

Berliner was himself again.

"The problem isn't tables," I said. "The problem is knowing."

"The problem is everything," said Berliner. "Like some guy stops me in the street. He says, 'Which way is the courthouse?' I look at my right hand. Then I say, because I know the other hand is left, 'Go left at the corner.' I need to see my right hand, you dig?"

"If the courthouse was a right turn, you'd look at your left hand?"

"No, man. I'd look at my cock."

Terry said, "I've got something to say." He had to speak through Berliner's laughter.

I said, "Berliner, that was a sad story."

"It was," said Paul, looking at Berliner with admiration. "I know what you're talking about. It happened to me, too." He was trying to make up for his failure to understand Berliner earlier, trying to repair the break in their communion. Not so much a drug brother as a kid brother; he adored Berliner.

Terry frowned. He wanted to talk, but Berliner was laughing, Paul was brimming over, and I also wanted to talk. Then Paul was talking, pushing himself before us, lunging and tumbling into what happened to him, offering it to Berliner.

"I know what you mean, Solly. A woman likes you.

By contrast, you know Sheila doesn't. That also happened to me. It was the same thing, but the other way around. I mean I liked a certain woman. What happened is my wife's father died and she had to go to the funeral in Idaho. She'd be gone for two weeks. Two weeks is long. After a couple of days, I got lonely. I couldn't sleep, eat, nothing. I wanted her to come home. I phoned her and said I didn't like being alone. She said she wasn't in Idaho having fun. Her family was fighting over the estate. She was the only one who could be fair, the only one they trusted. She had to stay longer and that's that. Same day my boss tells me about this party. It's a fund raiser for a politician. Somebody from our firm has to be at the party, like to show the politician we are behind him. I say okay, I'll go. At the party I'm standing around trying to enjoy myself, but I don't know anybody. I felt more and more lonely. I miss my wife. Then this woman who works for the politician comes up to me and starts talking. She doesn't say it, but I could tell she picked me out because I looked the way she felt. She tells me she is looking for a house. I'm listening to her and I'm beginning to feel relieved. Somebody is talking to me. I don't want her to go away. Maybe I acted more interested than I was, but soon she's telling me that she lived with a man for years, with him and her two kids, but now they are breaking up and she needs her own house. First time I ever saw the woman and she tells me this. But it's a party. You tell a stranger what you wouldn't always tell a friend. After a while, I begin to get really interested. Hopeful, maybe. My wife was gone almost a week by then. I didn't even know when she was coming back. She kept saying there was another legal complication, another delay. So here I am at a party. The woman is telling me she looks for a house every day and can't find one. Always too expensive, or the neighborhood is wrong, or something is the matter with the house. This has been going on for a year now. She's still living with the man. He works nights, a short-order cook, but lately he's been out of work and they're sleeping in the same bed, and they hardly talk. Never touch. Her name is Molly. She's about thirty, thirty-five. Attractive. Maybe a little scrawny, a little tight and nervous. I could see she has problems. She's wearing a yellow dress and she has a yellow ribbon in her hair. Too bright. And her eyes are too big. She's talking like the thing with the house and man was happening to somebody but not her exactly. I got more interested and I was a little sorry for her. She has a nice figure, but she's wearing too much yellow, and her eyes look exploded, like she's going crazy searching for what flew away. Then I said I didn't believe she wanted to move out. She would have found a house if she wanted to move out. 'Why wouldn't I want to move out?' she says, very surprised, like she never thought of that. I told her it was obvious. She loves the man. She laughed. She says, 'If anything, he loves me.' She woke up one night, she says, and found him beating her. In her sleep, he jumped on her, crying like a kid and beating her. Then she asks me to talk about myself, but what was I going to say after that? My wife is out of town? I'm lonely? In no time we're talking about her again. I wasn't hopeful anymore. I never played around anyway. I was lonely, but playing around is not my style. A woman talks to me at a party. What is that supposed to mean? She loves me? I mean, I liked her. Maybe I wanted to go to bed with her, but she was too complicated. She can't find a house because a guy is beating her up in her sleep. Next thing, she'd be telling me about her spinal tap, her year in the rubber room. Then the party is starting to end. She offers me a ride. I say my car is parked two blocks away. She says she owes me for listening to her. Like it's funny. Like she's being funny to make up for the bad shit she told me. She says I was a nice guy, I did her a favor listening, and now I have to let her give me a ride to my car. I laugh and tell her all

right and we walk out together. We walk and we walk,
and every couple of blocks she has to stop, look
around, try to think. She can't remember where she
parked her car. 'I'm so embarrassed,' she says. An
hour later, when we walked about a mile, I'm beginning to understand why that guy beats her up. I'm beginning to think she doesn't even have a car, when she
spots it. 'Gloria!' she says. 'You were hiding from
me, weren't you. Bad car. Bad Gloria.' It's an old
Buick. Front seat like a couch. We get in. I don't show
her I'm a little disgusted. I'm still being a nice guy,
but now I really need a ride. I'm waiting. I notice she
isn't moving. I look at her. She is staring at me like
she was waiting for me to look at her. She says,
'Thanks.' I say, 'For what?' She says, 'You're a good
person.' I say, 'For listening to you? It was nothing.
I enjoyed it.' She says, 'No, it was not nothing. It was
really kind of you.' I say, 'You're welcome, but it was
nothing.' She says, 'No. Don't say that. It was wonderful of you. I want to say thanks. I'm grateful to you,
Bill.' I say, 'Paul.' Her face twists. She looks frightened. 'Forgive me,' she says, 'I'm so sorry I called
you Bill.' I say, 'Paul sounds like Bill. Almost the
same name. Anybody could make that mistake and
who cares? Call me Bill, call me Shithead, if you
want.' She starts to cry. 'I hurt you,' she says, 'didn't

I? How could I have done that.' Man, I made a little joke. But she doesn't see it as a joke. I put my hand on her leg. Like to show her everything is okay. I just gave her a friendly touch. Soon as she feels my hand, she comes sliding across the seat to me. What I wanted, right? I mean it is, but it isn't. Not like this. Too weird, but we're into heavy petting, like high-school kids. Then we're trying to do the whole works in the front seat. My head is banging against the steering wheel and it's getting very hot in the car, but once you get started there is no going back. I was excited by the idea, maybe, not the thing. The thing didn't work, anyway. It was over in three minutes. I felt terrible. She looks happy. She was shining. You'd have thought we had a real good time. She says, 'Let's get something to eat. Let's have dinner or something.' She is shining, full of energy, ready to start the evening. I was sitting there with my pants around my ankles. My dick looks crushed. Like somebody stepped on it. She sees I don't feel happy and she says, 'Next time it will be better.' I told her I had to go home now, but I would phone her. She says, 'You promise to phone me? Will you phone tomorrow?' I said I would, I promise. She drove me to my car. The next day, like I promised, I phoned her. Not to make a date, but I promised so I phoned. Right away she says, 'Why don't you come over to my place.' Instead of saying no, I say, 'What about your friend, the guy you live with?' She says, 'I do what I want. The man doesn't decide who I see or don't see.' I said, 'All right. I'll come over.' She tells me she lives in Oakland, gives me directions. Her voice is shining. I could almost see her, the way she looked in the car. I remembered what she said about the next time. I'm excited, but on my way over to her house I had second thoughts. This was stupid. I didn't want to do this. She is attractive and everything, but I'm driving along, getting close to her place, and I ask myself, 'Do you want to do this?' The answer is no. The thing in her car was not good. There was also the man. She called him 'the man.' What was I doing getting mixed up with them? I didn't like the idea of the man one bit. I turned around, started driving back, thinking I would go to a movie. Go to sleep. Phone my wife and tell her she has to come home no matter what. Two minutes later I turn around again, thinking this is more stupid. I said I would go to her place and I ought to go. Nothing to worry about. It's simple. A little companionship. I'd have a good time. Everybody does it. I didn't do it, but why not? Was something wrong with me? I could do it. So what if I didn't want to do it? That was no fucking reason not to do it. I drove to her house mad at myself, but like feeling definite. I go stomping up the steps to her door. I ring the bell. I'm thinking she will open the door wearing a nightgown, shining at me. We will embrace and do it. Both of us will feel joy. I don't know what her living room looks like, but I'm imagining we will do it there, on the floor. My heart is beating so strong that my shirt is jumping. I can hardly breathe. The door opens and I almost shit in my pants. It's the man. The porch light is hitting him. I see everything. He's got a broomstick head with nose holes, but no nose and no chin. His neck comes to his lower lip. He is wearing thick glasses, so thick it's like they make him blind. He says, 'You must be Paul.' I hear kids laughing and music from a TV set. His voice is warm and friendly. He's wearing an apron and carrying a wooden ladle, as if he's in the middle of cooking dinner. A cigarette is in the other hand. He takes a drag, looking at me through his goggles, and his lower lip comes about to the middle of the cigarette. His knuckles get sticky with spit. He says, 'Molly went to buy some whiskey, I think. I heard her tell the kids that Paul is coming over. You're welcome to come inside and wait.' I said, 'Oh, thank you. Please tell her I'll be right back.' Like I rang the doorbell to say I would be right back. When I get to my car I am so relieved that I think I will sit here, in my car, with the windows rolled up and the doors locked, for the rest of my life. I will never move again. I could understand why she couldn't find a house. I couldn't explain it. I could understand. Don't ask me to explain. I mean the man is wearing an apron. He has no nose. I don't even want to think about it. I saw her coming up the street hugging a grocery bag, hurrying, almost running. I slunk down. She went by without seeing me. I don't remember starting my car, but I got home in about five minutes. I must have done fifty on College Avenue. I didn't notice nothing."

Kramer said, "Anybody want some coffee?"

Berliner said, "Your pants around your ankles. I see it. I see it, man. You're sitting in the car with your pants around your ankles. That's a scream."

"Yeah," said Paul, looking at Berliner with a dim light of pleasure, sharing the scream.

"But why is your story like mine?"

"The cars."

"The cars?"

"She was sad. We went to her car. Then she was happy."

Berliner said nothing. Paul glanced at me. "No?"

"Maybe it is," I said, not knowing what is or isn't.

Berliner muttered, "She used you."

"Yeah. You're right. That's what I mean."

Cavanaugh said, "You shouldn't tell that story. There are stories nobody should tell."

"It's what happened. It's not a story. My wife left town and this woman laid me."

"Cavanaugh is kidding you," said Terry. "I'm glad you told it. What happened when your wife got home?"

"Your pants around your ankles," said Berliner, laughing. "It's a scream."

"I was happy when my wife got home. She said, 'You horny or something?' She expected me to be mad at her. She said, 'You horny? It's only been two weeks.' I said, 'Let's go to bed.' She said, 'It's the middle of the day. The house is a mess.' I said, 'Please.' She said, 'I have too much to do.' We spent the afternoon in bed. I was happy she was home and that's the truth."

"You weren't lonely anymore," I said.

Paul began fixing himself another marijuana. "When she's around, I don't have to try to live."

"Well, I don't know about you guys," said Cavanaugh, smiling and surly, as if Berliner and Paul, in their stories, had reproached him. "But I love to do it. I've driven to other cities, my pickup loaded with camping equipment. Sarah thinks I'm going to the Snake River to fish. I'm driving to Denver to fuck."

Paul said, "You know how to live. Drive to Denver . . . That's cool. If I tried it, I'd have an accident, go off a cliff or something."

Terry, looking at Cavanaugh, said, "They used to call a person like you oversexed. You'd drive to Denver? Must be twenty hours. More."

"It's fun."

"Driving to Denver?"

"The sex."

Terry scowled. "It makes you laugh?"

Cavanaugh laughed. Berliner laughed at him.

Terry said, "Sex is serious, but I'm sure it could be other things. For imbeciles it could be fun. Not for a man like you, Cavanaugh."

"It's fun," said Cavanaugh.

Berliner shouted, "Paul got his dick crushed. That's fun." Laughing teeth and gums, his head snapped on a whiplike spine.

Cavanaugh, lifting his wineglass, talked to it. "Life," he said. Then said, "Life is thirst." Nobody was listening. He drank his thirst.

SIX

Terry frowned and smiled. Big head; big face, like the map of a nation. Room for antithetical feelings. The eyelids fluttering, as if assailed by gnats, suggested embarrassment, uncertainty. The spill of his lower lip was amusement. A loosening—submission to Berliner's raucous, licentious laughter—checked by small clutches of muscle, like tiny fists, at the corners of his mouth. Fluttering above, clutching below. What to call this expression? Maybe every combination in a face doesn't have a name. But he'd name it himself. He was gathering toward speech, like a man about to rumba, waiting to feel the beat. From Terry

—round, square, bulky—I expected definitive matter. Truth pressed by flesh. He looked only at Berliner. Berliner quit laughing. Terry was a doctor. People listen to them.

"I married young. I didn't know much about women."

He'd said this earlier, when Berliner left the room. Terry wanted him to hear it now, his motto. In his medical office, I supposed, diplomas hung on the walls. Like the silk shirt on his back. Credentials. Manifestations of his presence in the world, as distinguished from your own. More to the point, he was changing the mood in Kramer's dining room. He wouldn't begin amid the brainless residue of Berliner's laughter. Too much self-respect.

"I also met a woman like yours, Berliner. I was married then, working in an emergency room, thirty-six-hour shifts, twice a week. Nicki wanted me to do something else, maybe private practice. But the money was good and I had plenty of free time. The emergency room wasn't in a nice neighborhood. I saw knife wounds. Men came in with things stuck up their assholes. Cucumbers. Coke bottles. An armed guard was always at the door."

Berliner nodded, as if hammered lightly behind the head, to show his appreciation of real life. His mouth was slightly open, waiting for the woman, not laughing.

"It was another medical education. Good for me, I thought. Then, late one night, a gorgeous Latino appears in high heels and a tight short skirt. Also jewelry —rings, glass baubles—like this emergency room is her place for dancing. Her hair is black black. Moist-looking; gleaming like hot tar. She is young, confident, daring. She is the boss. I heard that already in her heels coming toward me. Hard linoleum floor. Bare halls. She walked like drumsticks. She made a racket."

Berliner smiled. This drama tickled him. Bare halls, hard floor, gorgeous Latino making her entrance, and here is Terry, young doctor, healing afflictions of the night. I looked at Terry's shirt. Could anyone in that shirt—subtle mauve expensive silk—care much for other people? It occurred to me I wanted his shirt.

"She sits, crosses her legs. Superior legs. Then she takes out a cigarette and offers me one. I didn't accept. The nurse might have noticed. It wouldn't look right, I thought, smoking with a patient. Her in particular. I said, 'What's your problem?' Now it makes me laugh."

His voice lifted; didn't laugh. This was life. You laugh at it theoretically.

"She says the doctors in the emergency room make

arrangements with her for prescriptions. I say, 'Yes?'
Not an appropriate response, but I didn't know what
she was talking about. She's cool, matter-of-fact, as if
I do know in a general way. 'It's the tradition,' she
says. I say, 'Yes? What's your problem?' She repeats
herself about arrangements, negotiations. Tells me
this is not uncommon. Then asks would I mind if she
shuts the door. Nobody was out there except the nurse.
I said, 'If you'll feel more comfortable, shut the
door.' She does. Then she assures me I can phone
doctors in L.A. who will vouch for her. Names names
and specialties. Urology. Radiology. I begin to understand. She hasn't come for a diagnosis. Nothing is the
matter. She wants to make an exchange. Do business.
The door is shut, but she is whispering."

"She's like the woman I met?" said Berliner.

"Yes. She had an effect on me. I learned from her
about myself."

"But the one I met liked me."

"May I go on?"

"Go on."

"She wants to do business. For certain prescriptions, she'll do whatever I want, at my convenience, in
a regular way. 'Anything,' she says. She takes a date
book from her purse. As if it's all settled, she asks,
'What are your hours?' "

"Man, she's nothing like the one I met."

Cavanaugh said, "Shut up, Solly."

Terry said, "Yes, she is. Listen to me. This was a difficult moment. They don't teach this in medical school. It is overlooked, ignored, never mentioned."

"What's this, this, this?" said Berliner.

"What she called the tradition. What she said is 'not uncommon.' You know what I said? I said, 'Go away.' She gave me a look I still feel. Like I'm a sick nut from the street. She says, 'You need a doctor, Doctor.' She turns, walks to the door, then looks back. To make sure she isn't dreaming. I say, 'Go away or I'll call the cops.' She opens the door, walks out. I'm standing there in my doctor outfit, my little office, by myself. She was going away. I myself chased her out. I felt grief. For this grief I was wearing a plastic name tag. For this grief they gave me instrument trays, prescription pads, and people called me Doctor. I cried out, 'Wait, you forgot something.' She kept on walking. She didn't hear me. I didn't cry out again. I'd done enough; too much. I was trembling. Then the nurse says, 'Wait. Doctor wants you. You forgot something.' She stopped. I was standing at my desk, looking down the hall at her. She looked back, waiting for me to speak. I had to say something, tell her what she forgot. The nurse was listening. I said, 'Your prescription.' Like a fool. I didn't mean it. But too late. She starts back, heels knocking, jewelry bouncing. She is putting on an act for the nurse with her whole body, laughing, shaking her head. Oh, it's so funny that she forgot her prescription. She came back inside the office and, without asking me, shut the door. You don't have to shut the door to write a prescription. It must have looked bad. I was locked in, and if the truth were known, I loved it. Now she wasn't so damned gorgeous. Now there was something at stake. I could see flaws. She was arrogant, hot, suffocating meat. I couldn't even talk."

Berliner, half-smiling—a little disappointed, not disapproving—said, "All right, man," as if conceding the world. "What was her name?"

"I can't remember."

"Bullshit."

Terry smiled and conceded: "Mango."

"That's her name?"

"But the point is—"

"Mango," screamed Berliner, a vehement, exotic bird.

Taking yet another slice of pie, Terry said, "My com-
pliments to your wife, Kramer. She baked this with
her hips. Give her my applause."

The courtesy, grossly extended, was cruel. Maybe
Berliner's laughter had annoyed Terry; hence he
punished Kramer. Or he was embarrassed by his own
incontinence. In his story and at this table. Nobody
else was still eating. In the bones of the bald head
was a need to chew. The more he talked, the more
they needed to churn, crush, savor. Kramer seemed to
enjoy watching him, even to be grateful for the sight,
as if he recognized something in Terry he particularly
liked.

"Nancy will be delighted to hear what you said.

I'm positive she made this pie. There is more if you want."

Each word, like a vessel of liquid, was evenly and distinctly uttered not to spill. He struggled thus to contain his pride in Nancy's pie. A good generous host. His furniture, paintings, plants, ceramics, and tattoos bespoke a lust for accumulation, but he lusted also to give. He'd slept with hundreds of women. His generosity was oceanic, lusciously abundant, like his black hair. Styled precisely, too.

Paul, from an abyss of reflection, said, "Women like doctors."

Terry stopped chewing. "You mean my Latino?"

"Yeah."

"I had something she wanted. Prescriptions."

"Oh, come on."

"The truth. She bought drugs and sold them at a higher price. She'd done this for years, on and off. Ever since high school. She needed the money."

"Yeah, yeah. But you're a doctor. Women like doctors because they're real. Most men are losers."

"You think doctors can't be losers?"

"I'm saying only what that chick was after. It wasn't scrips, it was you. There are other ways of making money." He sounded resentful. Logic wasn't a nice way to talk to him.

"I saw her again. The rest was repetitions, complications. The meeting I like to remember. Pleasure is in the beginning."

"Courtship," I said, "in the emergency room."

"Indeed, courtship. Wooing." Terry grinned. "Mango and I became friends, or what you could call friends. I even loaned her money. Sometimes twice a week I'd drive to Martinez. She lived near an oil refinery. Farmhouse with a couple of acres. She grew chard, peas, tomatoes, artichokes—a talented gardener, can you believe it? She had chickens and rabbits, too."

"She wasn't a hooker?" said Berliner.

"Too original. She was an entrepreneur. Her name was Felicia Mango. She worked in a factory. No education. Her handwriting was moronic. Balloons instead of dots over the i's. Also heavy loops under the g's and y's, like testicles. But she could name all the local wild flowers. Fantastic memory. I'd recite a list of thirty numbers and she could repeat it with no mistakes, backwards. She made me swear I wouldn't tell anybody she could do this. She thought something was wrong with her. I said, 'You're a talented woman.' She pointed at me and laughed: 'You're a big nut.' I said she was gorgeous. She said, 'You're gorgeous, too. You don't have pimples. I got pimples.'"

"What do you mean 'friends'?" said Berliner. "You were fucking."

"Doctors or losers. Friends or fucking. Is there no other way to think? You know, I used to believe the wheel was the basis of Western civilization. Then I read, in a book about the history of machines, it was the principle of reciprocating motion. Not the wheel. Yes; no. Right; wrong. That's how we think, build a bridge, talk, walk. I was her friend. Sometimes we'd go for a drive, Berliner, and not fuck. I loaned her money and she paid it back. Once I helped change an elbow pipe in her toilet. I'm good with my hands. I was showing off. Pails of rusty water. Black nasty grease. I loved it. What bothered me was the sentiment. The idea. Me doing this for her. Afterwards in bed she was more affectionate than sexual. She asked questions about my wife. She wanted to know what Nicki looks like. Also does Nicki care if I see other women. Cavanaugh says he doesn't like kissing. Me, it was talking about my wife. I'd get depressed. She'd say, 'Tell me some numbers.' She knew it amused me, impressed me that she could repeat thirty numbers. After a while, it only broke my heart a little."

"But she was a friend," said Berliner. "To me—"

Cavanaugh interrupted. "Solly, it's not hard to understand. I was making it with a woman who always wanted to take pictures of me. Like I'd be on the crapper and the door flies open. Click. I'd be in the shower and the curtain rips away. Click, click. She has a hundred pictures of me washing my ass. I was her friend."

"Yes. Something like that," said Terry, looking doubtful even as he nodded yes, yes. "But I know Felicia was my friend because she stopped asking me for prescriptions. I offered. She got mad. She said she only takes from pigs. Others have less trouble in these situations than I do. She was a friend. But the truth is I don't go down on my friends. You see what I'm getting at?" He laughed heavily, as if the idea were funnier than the fact. "I used to be a political person, a lefty. I signed petitions, gave to good causes. Now, all of a sudden, I understood the meaning of alienation. A body lying next to me in bed was asking questions about my wife."

"A friend," said Berliner, as if repeating the word restored meaning. "Man, you are weird."

"He believes in the principle of reciprocating motion," I said.

"I'm a scientist. I don't like to kid myself too much. She was a body."

"Did she see other men?" I asked.

"She once phoned me at the emergency room. I

was knee-deep in blood and shit, but it was Felicia, so I ran to the phone. She asked if it's all right for her to have dinner with a jerk at the factory. Would I mind? Of course I didn't mind. I wanted her to see other men, though it worried me. If I carried bugs it would be a disaster."

"Your wife was a body, too," I said.

"Marriage should be monogamous. I believe this with all my heart."

"To prevent bacteria," said Paul. "I can dig that."

"To prevent the wife from becoming a body. It isn't a question of bacteria—though, naturally, I worried plenty about infections. I took precautions. Still, I worried. Sure enough, I got an infection. Don't ask me how. Maybe I wanted it. I had to phone Nicki's gynecologist. He'd been my professor in medical school and we both moved to California at the same time. It didn't make things easier. Nicki was seeing him for a problem with cysts. Which was convenient, but I had to go to his office, tell him the whole story. He was interested from a medical point of view. How did I get the infection? Was it a new, hybrid strain? It was plain clap. He was also sympathetic. The way he listened made me pity myself. He encouraged me to talk. I nearly cried, I felt so disgraced. I told him Nicki was on the verge of nervous collape, which was

crazy. Nobody who plays tennis, who jogs, who sleeps
nine hours a night, is nervous. I must have meant
myself, but I went on about poor Nicki. I told him
how she rushed out of the house in the middle of an
argument and drove away like a madwoman. How
once she didn't see the neighbor's dog sleeping in our
drive. She ran him over. I made her sound homicidal.
If she discovered she had clap, would she suppose it
came from her tennis racket? No; she'd do something
dramatic. He knew her, but he believed every word.
He asked if we shouldn't consult a psychiatrist. Think
about having her committed. For her own good. I had
a horrible picture of myself. A doctor gives his wife
clap and has her committed for her own good. I
wouldn't discuss it further. I could treat her myself, I
said, maybe slip drugs into her yogurt. But I had to
leave town for about ten days. I was helpless. He
promised to help me, to be discreet. We shook hands.
He patted me on the back. When I next phoned him,
he said, 'She's clean,' and hung up. No bill for services, only a sock in the ear. Maybe he was disappointed in me, but why he wanted to hurt my feelings I'll never know. Thank God Nicki didn't have
clap."

"*Praise the Lord!*" screamed Canterbury.

He smiled as if he intended more, but—screaming—
he'd shocked himself, lost the necessary presence of
mind. He quit. He was still. Blond clean pale stiff. A
smile in a floating head. Holiday colors below.

I wondered if Canterbury, mildly epileptic perhaps,
had had a seizure. A long moment passed. Everyone
staring at him. I was reminded of a student, a boy who
sat in a corner in back of the room, saying nothing
for weeks, and then, last day of class, cried out, got
everyone's attention, and was unintelligible. Like
Canterbury, he was there, but he wasn't here. One
needs a sense of the person, sometimes, to understand
even his simplest utterance. We don't hear words; we
hear ourselves, personally, speaking words. All night
he'd said virtually nothing. He wanted to be a zero,
but I had to see him, at least peripherally, every time
I looked up. He was there, across the table, practicing
invisibility. Now he'd burst with exasperation; abrupt
protrusion of inner life. Under the pressure of our
staring, he tipped back in his chair, making a picture
of sublime ease, and said, "Ignore me."

But he was strained, not easy. Meanings controlled
by no intention drifted from his features. The smile
lay in his lips like a feeling he didn't want to have.
Something precious, however. Very paradoxical. I
wondered if he was gay, literally thinking the word.

It brought delirious evanescence to mind, high thin spirits. Not much like Canterbury, but maybe he was gay in the sense of grim. I had gay friends at the university who were dismal. No reason to think any of this, or anything so personal to Canterbury. That's why I thought it. He wasn't of this company. He'd eaten like the rest of us and sat there listening, but produced no credentials.

"What are you talking about?" said Cavanaugh to be solicitous, but his size and the direct thrust of the question made him intimidating.

Insane, epileptic, gay, smiling, pale, Canterbury said, "I don't know."

He crossed and uncrossed his legs. A display of restless irrelevance, as if to say, Don't look at me, I'm not here, but look at me, I'm here thrashing in my chair, tipped way back, utterly relaxed. He looked precarious. I was uneasy. When it happened, I squealed like a girl.

Canterbury's hands were catching, slapping, losing the edge of the table as he fell back slowly, inevitably, then fast, arms flailing. There was a crash of wood and bones. I no longer saw him.

Had Berliner fallen, there would have been a festival of jeering and laughter. For Canterbury there was exquisite silence. He righted his chair. He sat in it again. Correctly erect, ready to resume, the smile in his face once more as though the event had already disappeared from human history. Kramer, with a judicious tone, said, "In my opinion, Harold is telling us to shut up."

He meant no joke. The remark came from his professional self, one who knew the reasons of things. Canterbury looked at Kramer fully and coldly, daring him to interpret the fall. Kramer didn't, but he looked back knowingly. He seemed to resonate implications. Canterbury took them like a stain. His ears reddened. Hairs, pressed by blood, radiated along the rims. A fine white contrasting haze. Even across the table from him, I could see it. He was furious.

"I dislike being analyzed. I resent it, Kramer. I'm not your patient or whatever you call them—clients?" Further objections collected, jammed in his neck. "I said to ignore me. Ignore me."

Kramer, hastening to comply, spoke softly. "Sure, man. Not everyone who hears our stories would like them. I wasn't making a judgment. I understand. You don't have to like the stories."

"Thanks. I've been sitting here afraid I had to like them."

There had been other ironical remarks. This had icy force. Mean. Bitchy. Kramer blinked, rubbed his wandering eye, and settled back, watching Canterbury. He too now wanted to be ignored, but Canterbury said, "Before you produce the entire philosophy of your psycho-science, let me say the stories are obscene. Oh, really, what difference does that make? The population of America is large. Who cares what anyone says about anyone else? No personal information is so peculiar that it doesn't apply to millions. You'd be out of business if things were otherwise. Isn't that true? An individual, a real individual with dignity, with self-respect, couldn't go to a therapist, could he? You see nothing but a stream of whining, sniveling creeps, don't you?"

"I never thought of my clients that way. Some are very individual. You should hear the shit they tell me. If that isn't individual, I don't know what is. Mainly, I do marriage and family counseling. Husbands and wives together. Sometimes with kids. I also see people alone. I don't know what you mean by individuals."

"Terry knows. He's a doctor. He knows he can talk all night about Mango and he isn't describing her any more than a million other women. She did what he wanted for prescriptions. She raised rabbits. So what? She'll be on TV tomorrow. She's nobody. She doesn't exist."

"Doesn't exist?" Terry poked his ribs under his right arm with his fork. "She has a supernumerary nipple. Here. How's that for peculiar?"

Canterbury's smile brightened with contempt. "Really? How about her teeth? Normal number?"

"Yes. Also a five-year-old son who lives with her ex-husband, a cripple. He was injured doing construction work. The compensation payments bought the house in Martinez. Felicia is nobody? I helped fill out her income-tax forms. At her kitchen table. Blue and white oilcloth, faded, cracked like old skin. Sticky. She exists. She sewed a button onto my jacket sleeve. For months I carried that button in my pocket. If she doesn't exist, how do you account for that button? I wouldn't have sewn it on myself. If I asked Nicki to do it, she'd have sewn it between my eyes."

At "eyes" Canterbury rolled his eyes, as if assaulted by moral idiocy.

"Oh, it's finally a matter of taste. This sort of talk makes me feel soiled. Lonely. I know I've been sitting here listening. I suppose I have a debt to the club. I should tell a story, too, or at least slander someone. But stories don't happen to me. I have an ordinary life. I don't know gorgeous Latinos who raise rabbits. Great loss for me, I'm sure. I should have gone home. I don't belong in this club."

Cavanaugh loomed at his end of the table, moun-
tainous, immobilized. Paul rolled no marijuana. Berliner muttered something, denied it, sighed. Terry
was bogged in his densities. He'd done his best and
failed. Kramer, sunk within his darkness, said, "People go to therapists because they have to. They're in
pain." He'd been dropped minutes ago, bleeding
heavily.

"Yes, get rid of their pain," said Canterbury.
"Throw it out. See what you're saying? No respect
for their own pain. Get rid of their pain and everything else goes with it. My wife had six years of psychoanalysis. I know what I'm talking about. She took
every stick of furniture. I came home one night to a
hollow house. She left a note saying, 'Dear, you can
keep the furniture. I've taken some of the duplicates.'
There was nothing. Not even a dish towel. I paid for
six years of psychoanalysis for her."

His wife?

I said, "Canterbury, you want to go home, but you
don't go home. You want to be ignored, but you fall
out of your chair."

"I have feelings. You guys sound like a bunch of
homos."

Berliner grabbed me around the neck, yanked me
toward him, kissed my cheek.

"Thanks, shmuck," I said, wiping my cheek with the back of my hand. Now I understood Canterbury. He wasn't gay. He was a critic, a perfect person. Kramer, clinging still to his therapeutic manner, fraught with reasonableness, said, "Nobody has an ordinary life, Harold. Not even you. It's not common for somebody's wife to disappear with all the furniture."

"I certainly do have an ordinary life. I drive to San Francisco in the morning. I drive back in the evening. I never pick up hitchhikers. I've never gotten a traffic ticket. As for the furniture, that was surprising; but I realized what it meant. She was leaving me. I think she made her point too strongly, but then she could also have burned down the house. It was still there, after all. She didn't take the doors and windows. They are detachable and they aren't without value. Do you know what it costs to have a door hung? But I don't really want to pursue this incident. I was saying something about psychoanalysis, that's all. If you think, after six years of psychoanalysis, my wife decided to leave me and ream out the house, it means I'm wrong about myself, well, that's your business. Think what you like. As far as I'm concerned, nothing happens to me. It never does. This men's club proves what I'm talking about. I come to the meeting and it turns out not to be a real men's club. Why aren't we doing anything physical?"

"Physical?" said Kramer.

"Of course. Aren't we supposed to *do* something? Something physical? All this talk, talk, talk. It's sick."

Berliner, smiling, said, "You never, you nothing. Too much, Harold. You must have a secret life. Confess, man. What do you do?"

"I'm a lawyer."

"Far out."

"Well, there's nothing secret about it. I sue people and defend them against suits. I should say corporate individuals. People can't afford the services of my firm. I read documents and write legal instruments. Occasionally, I'm required to travel. Then I'm in some hotel room or talking to a judge, clarifying arguments. The work is hectic. Full of anxieties. One of the senior partners collapsed recently during a conference."

"That's a story," said Berliner.

"Good. I told it, paid my debt to the club. Quentin had a heart attack and died. Quentin Cohen. You may know that he invited me here."

"Quentin?" said Berliner, standing up as if he'd been called from another room.

"Haven't you noticed he isn't here? I suppose others didn't show up. Perhaps they're all dead."

Berliner, mouth open, lips hardly moving, spoke as if his words came from yesterday or tomorrow. "Quentin is dead?"

"Yes. He fell down at a conference."

"He fell down?" Berliner put a hand through his hair and, as if imitating words, said, "He fell down." He needed another fact, something to help assimilate the news. Sufficiency settled in Canterbury's features. His eyes, lit by inner principle, looked bluer. That he had no more to say made him terrific. Berliner waited in vain. Canterbury was stone. Then, as if wheedling with fate, Berliner said, "But Quentin wasn't a sick guy. We had lunch a couple of weeks ago. He ate lasagna. We used to play poker, go to the track. He had plans. A trip to Acapulco." He sat again and said, "You see it?"

"A dozen people saw it. Lawyers. A stenographer. Quentin was speaking when he fell and hit the table. We caught him before he slid to the floor. We pulled him onto the table, on his back."

"Then?"

"Berliner, you're harassing me. Coins and keys spilled out of his pockets. Drool was at the corner of his mouth. What do you want to hear?"

"He was my friend."

"Well, I'm sorry. I didn't know him intimately. He had a speech impediment."

"That's right."

"I mention it. His chief physical feature. I was always conscious of it. Perhaps if I'd known him better I wouldn't have been. When he invited me here, it was an overture. He wanted to be closer. His secretary, cleaning out his desk, found a note he'd written to himself, saying to remind me of this meeting. She gave it to me a week ago. After his death. I hadn't gone to his funeral. In a sense, I'm here to pay my respects. Easier than a funeral. It was very terrible, the coffee cups all knocked over. What can I tell you? Somebody untied his shoelaces to help circulation. Quentin's socks were mismatched. One was brown as the salad bowl. See, along the outside. That brown. The other was white. Oddly indecorous, even rather shocking. The socks made him look clownish; vulnerable. He was probably distressed that morning. He had to speak in public. The prospect might have troubled him. His speech impediment. Squishy, sucking sound, like walking in wet grass. I never had a good idea of it. He spoke so quickly always. As though to disguise it or keep your attention on his next word, and he'd tip his head back when he spoke, as if pull-

ing himself above his mouth, away from it, and his
eyes watched you so closely. He watched what you
were listening to—his sense or his speech impediment.
I used to receive strange phone calls at home. At any
hour. A man's voice. He'd whisper. It frightened me.
Then, one day, I wasn't even thinking about it and I
realized the man was Quentin. I was positive. His
voice came through the whisper. Something came
through, the faintest something. Why would Quentin
do that? I never mentioned it to him, but after I knew,
I felt he knew that I knew."

"You never mentioned it?"

"Not to him. I discussed it with the other partners,
of course. That didn't do Quentin much good."

"What did he say on the phone?"

"It doesn't make any difference—the disturbing
thing was the whisper."

"You knew what he was saying?"

"He said the same thing always. Harold, how's
your cock?"

"Quentin said that?"

"I'm positive."

"But with his speech impediment," I said, "didn't
you have some idea it was him right away?"

"No. He whispered. Besides, people don't sound
exactly like themselves on the telephone. We don't

look like ourselves in photographs, either. We're merely recognizable, for better or worse. On the phone voices are thinned. Purified. The wires do it. For some it's a wonderful improvement. People complain so about modern technology. Depersonalizing and all that. As though there were something wonderful about the real person. My wife, for example. After six years of analysis, she finds out who she really is—a greedy little furniture thief. Well, Quentin came into himself on the telephone. His real self. His freedom."

Kramer stood up. "Who wants coffee? I think I'll put on coffee. The women bought Brazil, Kona, and Uganda. I can mix it up. How do you guys like it?"

"Sit down," said Berliner.

Kramer, at the kitchen door, stopped, about to push it open. "Let's have some coffee. Doesn't anyone want some coffee?"

Berliner slammed the table with his fists, shouting, "What is this coffee shit? Harold is talking. We came here to talk, not to drink some coffee. You want some fucking coffee, Kramer? Make some for yourself. Shove some up your ass."

Kramer walked back and leaned across the table toward Berliner, as if about to slide through the plates and grab his neck. The tattooed forearms had a lethal, serpentine gleam. He spoke, again with excess control, this time menacing, and he didn't blink. His eyes were locked open.

"Maybe you didn't hear what Harold said. I'll tell you what he said. He said our club is a fucking funeral. He said he came here to pay his respects to the dead. Mr. Lasagna with the speech problem and funny socks. Meanwhile, since Harold is here, he is doing us a big favor, which is to improve our morals. You know what I mean? He explained to me what I do for a living is a bunch of shit. Did you hear that? I thought you were my friend, Solly. Maybe I was wrong about you. Maybe I ought to kick your ass."

"Try it," said Berliner, lunging up, hair like thrashing salt, green eyes blown wide. "Come on. Come on."

"Wait a minute," cried Paul. Cavanaugh was moving around the table toward Kramer. I thought to grab Berliner, but he was fixed where he stood, legs trembling in his trousers, fists ready. Beside Kramer, Cavanaugh stood hugely, raising his arms as if to shed rays of peace. "Think of your friends," he said. "I love you guys. How will I feel if you start hitting? Think of your friends."

Kramer's eyes were on Berliner, hard, responsible to nothing like thought.

Canterbury rose. "It's my fault. I did it. I was

sitting here and I fell and said things. I caused the trouble. If you hit someone, hit me."

His smile came bearing wretchedness and hope to his white face.

Kramer said, "Fuck it," dropped into his chair, sighed.

Cavanaugh lowered his arms, then walked away slowly to his chair.

Kramer slumped, his head twenty pounds of black pout. I heard Berliner's breathing tear his throat. Paul looked at his hands, automatically beginning to roll a marijuana, a fat one to clog all synapses. Canterbury remained standing, glancing around the table, trying to find something to say. He seemed very isolated standing there, as if abandoned by all of us, far away, lonely as a pole. Kramer didn't even want to hit him. Then, inspired by sheer desperation, Canterbury said, "Terry, you were talking. What happened to what's her name? You were about to tell us, weren't you?"

"Me?" said Terry.

"Deborah Zeller," I said.

"Yeah," said Paul. "What about Deborah Zeller? She used to taste your food."

Listless, quick, scattered—somehow Terry began talking. He had no heart for it, but it was apparent he wanted to redeem the club. He watched our faces, measuring the interest in Deborah Zeller. Berliner's breathing was so loud I wondered if he could hear Terry. Kramer slumped, chin in hand; he studied the grain in the tabletop. He didn't give a damn about Deborah Zeller. His pleasure in the evening had been ruined. He was bitterly pissed off. But I gave a damn. I showed Terry an attentive face. Deborah Zeller was no mere name to me. I knew her. Not to say hello to in the street, of course, but if I were at a party and a woman said, "Hi, I'm Deborah Zeller," I'd have responded extravagantly, probably embarrassing both of us, the way one behaves with somebody famous, who exists immensely for others. Here comes Deborah Zeller, so famous I could virtually taste her as Terry talked. I tried to show him all this, how I flew ahead of his words, acquiring his sense of the woman only against my own, which in fact was nothing but romance and anticipation. It gave way slowly, surrendering to Terry's voice, his intention. He talked not for me. Not even for the club now. He talked the way he talked, a rhythm of authority in his sentences. The big round head—bald except for sandy fluff beside the ears—looked shaped from within by invincible power. A considerable bone with hazel eyes, bludgeon nose, full flexible mouth, talking of Deborah Zeller.

Confidently. Berliner's breathing became less loud and then I ceased to hear it. Even Berliner, in his fury, was listening. I felt reassured.

Paul, with quick skinny fingers, perfected his marijuana, a token of his staying here, his willingness to listen.

Canterbury, stiff again, sat like a man facing into wind.

Cavanaugh refilled his wineglass. He, too, was here.

Kramer slumped.

Terry talked.

"... at the university for years, like a faculty member, except she was in one department, then another. 'I took professors,' she said, 'not courses.' You know the type? Excellent student. Only she starts a dissertation in anthropology, then reads philosophy and wonders about going to law school; meanwhile, she applies for the program in business administration. Nervous; smokes. Never inhales, just smokes, smokes. Talks her head off, too. If you clear your throat or glance away from her eyes, she stops and says, 'What?' She was familiar with advanced work in half a dozen fields, and then—no goodbye—she takes a job with

an insurance company and begins to speculate in real
estate. She also had telephones with a computer hook-
up in her apartment. So she could play the commodi-
ties market. Her father's full-time work. She did it
as a hobby. No real respect for any career. How
could she have respect? Praise, high marks, fellowships—suddenly she's making a lot of money. The
only criticisms came from her father. She phoned him
to say she was worth a million on paper. He said,
'I'm delighted to hear you are thirty years old and
without a husband. Listen to me for once. Come back
to New York. Be with real people.' He depressed
her. 'I'm twenty-eight,' she said, 'not thirty.' I never
offered opinions about her life. What if she acted on
them? I'd be responsible, no? Besides, I admired her
brains and energy. I approved of her, envied her—
at least in the beginning. An extremely busy woman
who had time for dance classes and a Marxist study
group. Bay Area Women on the Left. She herself
organized the group. It met once a month in her
apartment. She assigned readings in Marx, gave a
talk, led the discussion. Another group she organized,
the Anacreontic League of Women, would fly to different cities to eat in fine restaurants. Whatever she
enjoyed tended to become a group. Lobster, pasta,
Karl Marx. If she wanted to swim across San Fran-

cisco Bay, eighty-five women would jump into the water behind her. Her father would yell criticisms from the shore. Me, I'd be rowing behind with no opinions, but full of admiration. Plenty of people would be involved. Her address book was thick as a dictionary. Her phone never stopped ringing. She had an answering machine that said 'Hi. Debbie Zeller speaking. I really want to talk to you, but I can't right this minute . . .' She was always busy. Her whole body—fingers, mouth, hair, feet—was busy. She was never bored.

"I met her through Nicki. When the divorce was final, Nicki started phoning every night, usually to talk about Harrison, her boy friend. Why do women treat me this way? Because I'm bald, I think. I make a simple, basic impression. Anyhow, she phoned with a story about a woman at the tennis club. Nicki was sitting on a bench waiting for her partner when this woman asks if she'd like to warm up, hit a few back and forth. Nicki agreed. Just hitting a few, this woman begins slamming to the corners. Nicki said, 'I was running my ass off.' She begins slamming back. Soon it was obvious Nicki could wipe her out. The woman quits, runs up to the net. 'Hi, I'm Debbie.' Her exuberance was overwhelming. 'She kept touching me,' said Nicki. 'Mad to be my friend or something.' Nicki is a reserved type, a little shy. No defense against this kind of approach. When the woman invited her to the study group, Nicki said yes, she'd definitely be there. She wasn't the least interested, she had doubts about the woman, but she said yes. So she asked if I would go with her. Harrison wanted no part of it. She didn't want to go alone. She couldn't not go at all. She was allowed to bring a friend, even a man. I said okay, I'd go. It turned out I was the only man. About fifteen women were in Deborah's living room when we arrived. Others came later. I hoped a man would walk in, but none did. When everyone was seated, Deborah introduced Nicki to the women and said she was a fantastic tennis player. Nicki had to stand up and introduce me. She was blushing and trembling. I, at least, had political views and I'd been to many such meetings. Finally Deborah started things officially. She gave a talk about Marx's idea of money. She made references to his work, early and late, and said he wasn't a metaphysician, economist, or visionary, but a first-class businessman. She kept glancing and smiling at Nicki as if she hoped to impress her, but I was the one who was impressed. I was knocked out. When she finished, I applauded. Nicki was relieved when the discussion was over and we could make our exit. She said Deborah was obviously bright, but too aggressive for her taste, and the way she dressed was awful. 'Did you see how short her skirt was? Years out of style.' Well, Deborah has a dancer's legs. Exceptional definition. Each muscle an independent dynamo. Later I found out she didn't think her legs were sexy, only delightful to contemplate. But when she walked down the street, hoodlums whistled and made sucking noises. She seethed with anger. I said, 'Don't wear short skirts.' She got angrier. She said, 'Women are more attractive than men. Even to each other. They enjoy looking at each other.' This was our second or third date. The first was after the study group. Deborah phoned the next morning. I was very surprised. Also frightened. She said she was leaving town. Would I like to have a drink with her before she goes? You know what I said? It makes me writhe to think of it. I said, 'Yes, thank you.' There was no reason to be frightened. Alone, Deborah was a little girl. When she sat on a couch, she flopped. I had to see not only her legs but also her underpants. She'd flop and begin a conversation, her knees a yard apart, her eyes on your eyes, as if she had no crotch. She could make money and lecture on Marx, but I had to look at her underpants. Her face was also something to look at. Close-together little eyes. They seemed never to miss your meaning, maybe to understand more than you intended. She'd say, 'To spend most of one's life thinking about money is intellectually degrading. Do you agree with this idea?' She never lectured when we were alone. She asked what I thought about this or that, then she'd ask why, then she'd repeat what I said and develop it. No phony style, either. She'd make me feel my depths. As I was saying, she had close-together little eyes. A slightly hooked nose, wide mouth, sharply turned heavy lips, and fierce overbite. Extreme face. Fundamentally African, but white, really white skin. Some would say too dramatic, too keen. I wouldn't argue, but it was an exciting face. Dark wiry hair and a fine long neck. Fine wrists and fingers. Very sensitive. Looking at her sometimes, I'd have a rush of pleasure. I'd laugh. Give her a hug. She'd say, 'You like me?' Not coquettish. Curious. Really curious. She said other men reacted similarly. 'Usually the blonds,' she said. She understood, but she didn't. It upsets me to talk about her, but I'm going on and on. You know why? Because of Harold. Every time I remember another detail, I think Harold doesn't believe me. I feel like I'm talking to a lie detector. I wanted to tell only one incident with Deborah and look, look what I've done. I'm producing a saga. Because of you, Harold."

Canterbury, already stiff enough, stiffened more.

I wondered if he'd been beaten as a child. He said, "Finish the story. Please."

"The story? I haven't begun the story."

"It couldn't have been so terrible as you think."

"It was terrible. I'm upset, really upset talking about her. You know what I'd like to do? I'd like to phone her. I have a pair of her earrings. She left them at my house one night. I should have mailed them to her long ago. I think this every day and I don't mail them. What do you suppose it means?"

"Nothing at all. Tell us why you're upset," said Canterbury. He seemed anxious to get out of sight. "Is it because you didn't marry her?"

"It wouldn't have lasted. I don't know why I'm upset. Maybe it ended too suddenly. Before I was ready. Maybe I'm nervous, that's all. The idea makes me nervous. The way relations between people fail, you'd think they get together to break apart and have something to talk about. Nothing to say about a successful relationship, is there? Who would want to listen? As for marriage, it's a still life. Like this table of plates and glasses. Doesn't move. You run into an old friend, you shake hands, you say, 'What's happening?' He says, 'I got married last month.' Your heart sinks. Poor guy. Not only is nothing happening, but he'll soon be miserable. 'Wonderful,' you say.

You're already dying to get free of him. Not that you
don't like him, but it's terrible to stand there lying—
that is, unable to say truly what you're doing. How
you're having six affairs, planning a trip to Rome,
and you bought a new Porsche. He wants you to
come to dinner. You'd love to come to dinner and meet
his wife, but you can't think when. You'll phone him,
you say. He pleads with you not to forget. You promise, but you'll never phone. Never. You'd sooner phone
the city morgue. Look, I'll be completely honest. I
can't stand couples. I hope none of your wives ever
invites me to dinner. So why am I upset? Deborah
and I wouldn't have gotten married. Neither of us
really wanted it. She had too much to do. I'd just
been divorced. When I woke up alone, really alone,
the first time in ten years, I was in a narrow bed in the
little suite for doctors at the emergency room, and I
was happy. You know, I looked at white walls and I
was happy. White walls, a TV set, a small cabinet, a
narrow bed. It was abundancy. My clothes were in a
suitcase in a closet and that's where I wanted them to
be. Later I bought a house. Ten rooms. All mine. So
why am I upset? I was still seeing my former wife
during the whole thing with Deborah. I talked about
Nicki with her. With Nicki I talked about Deborah.
If a complication arose with one, I could phone the

other and discuss it. Maybe I miss Deborah. If so,
what do I miss? Her face? Her legs? Other things,
too. She could sing. I'm a sucker for singing women.
You should see my record collection. Almost ex-
clusively singing women, from all over the world.
Every major race is represented. I remember one
night after a movie, driving home, the two of us, she
started to sing a blues. 'Brother, can you spare a
dime . . .' Naturally, a money blues, but I wasn't
listening to the theme. I drove slowly, hoping she
wouldn't quit singing. I had gooseflesh. I think she
didn't even know she was singing. You can love best
what people have no idea about themselves. Maybe
nobody ever praised her voice. She told me it was
noticed, when she was a kid, that she had musical
talent, but her father discouraged her from taking
piano lessons. 'You can play by ear,' he said, 'so study
mathematics, languages. Why waste money learning
what you can already do?' He never praised her voice.
Regarding that, she was innocent. She opened her
mouth to sing. Beauty flowed out. She didn't even
know. She didn't bring her big brain down on it. She
let it happen, like a spell. As if there were two of her.
One waited in silence until the other subsided. Then
she sang. I had a dream about her voice, but in the
dream I felt no pleasure. I remember it now. Every-

thing connects for me now. Deborah was on the ground, on her back. I was kneeling beside her head, saying, 'Deborah, tell me who to get in touch with. Hurry, hurry.' She was languid, wan-looking. A strange style for her, but in dreams you see the truth of a person. She was dying. I begged her to speak. 'Tell me who to call.' She said, 'Ginger, Mary, Tanya, Hortense, Helen, Nettie, Sally, Rosa, Franny . . .' I said, "Wait.' I took a scrap of paper from my wallet, started scribbling the names. She said, 'Billie, Millie, Tillie . . .' Hundreds of names. I was soon writing on my flesh. I'll say one thing. She yelled in bed. 'Look, look at me.' I didn't mind, but I was always shocked. She had a passion for publicity. No, I don't mean that. I mean she had a desire to multiply things. Give her a dollar, she made it thousands of dollars. If she had pleasure, I doubled its value by looking. What didn't multiply was nothing. I don't consider myself so different. I had a wife, then a wife and a lover, then a former wife, a former lover, and Deborah. Still it wasn't the same. Deborah had mirrors all over her apartment. Not sick mirrors, like over the bed, but little ones, big ones, round ones in corners or in the middle of a wall, so you'd always be catching sight of yourself. Also photos of herself on the walls. She wasn't vain. She lacked some crucial evidence. As for the incident, the one thing, one little thing I meant to tell you about . . . I'm still ashamed of it. I'll be brief. Harold has infected me with doubts. The more I say, the more uncertain I feel. Deborah exceeded herself in everything. I do the same, talking about her. She fixed on everything and nothing fixed her, you know what I mean?

"We were having dinner with some doctors in San Francisco. About ten of us, including wives and girl friends. I'd joined a gourmet society for doctors. Ordinarily, I don't see doctors socially. They talk about their condominiums in Texas and Hawaii. Plenty of real estate is financed by malignant tumors. Ask Berliner. Maybe I joined to impress Deborah, show her doctors know food. The dessert I ordered that night was strawberries under flaming chocolate. Good as this pie almost. I was not just eating it, I was committing it to memory. Deborah noticed. She gave me looks of approval, like to say how much she enjoyed my happiness. But what does she do? Takes her fork, sticks it into my dessert—without asking permission— and hacks away a piece for herself. Many things about this woman I admired. But nobody sticks herself between my plate and my mouth. She hacked away a piece, shoves it straight into her mouth. Deep. Almost to her lungs. I was looking with disbelief."

A look of disbelief entered Terry's face. He held it, letting us appreciate it. His brows lifted, his mouth hung.

"She looked back at me, rolling the piece of dessert around, a bulge in one cheek, a bulge in the other, and she is smiling as if we're sharing this piece of delicious dessert. I felt a surge of hatred. Isn't that terrible? It's what I felt. All her qualities, everything about her, converged for me in this moment. This was Deborah Zeller. Her fellowships, her million dollars, her groups, her mirrors, and my food in her mouth. Well, fuck you, I thought."

"What did you do?" said Paul. He listened visibly, the moment tearing at his features, hurting him. An outstanding appreciator.

Terry said, "Get the picture. Close-together eyes and dark wiry hair like a million bees. Her face projects from the middle of it, leaps at you. This face, these eyes, leaping at me, was eating my dessert."

"I get it, man. What did you do?"

"I kicked her under the table."

"No shit."

"She yelped. She tried to wiggle back, but her chair was caught in the rug."

"Wow."

"I kicked her again. She stabbed her fork under

the table at my foot. I was wearing thin Italian shoes.
She could have pushed the fork right through. I got
up, left the table, went home. It was the last time I
saw her."

Terry licked the tip of his index finger, pressed it
down on scraps of pie at the rim of his plate, nibbled
the scraps from the tip of his finger, mumbling, "I'm
ashamed. Also guilty." Perspiring along the upper
lip, mumbling, nibbling, he nailed down his conscience.

Kramer lifted from his slump, chuckling. "What a
bitch. What a bitch."

"You know her?" asked Terry.

"No. Why should I know her?"

Terry shrugged and picked up his fork. "Maybe
she was one of your clients."

"Yeah," cried Berliner. "Maybe you gave her some
coffee."

"Maybe I'll kick your ass," yelled Kramer, coming
out of his chair, arms forward, pouring across the
table through dishes and glasses to seize Berliner's
shirt front, both of them going over, dragging the
table after them. Plates and bottles and bowls spilled
to the floor, smashing. My plate hit my lap. I jumped
up, the plate falling, smashing with the others.

Kramer and Berliner grappled on the floor, grunting,
twisting, rolling over each other. It looked bad. They
were laughing. It still looked bad. They had wanted
to kill each other. Now they were hugging on the floor.
Better than killing, I'm sure, but there had been that
rush across the table and their bodies toppling with the
food and glass. For an instant, I had been filled with
fright and violence, feelings difficult to dismiss, but
they had no object, so I stood like a dolt, nothing to do
but gape. Then I noticed Terry holding his fork in
the air, talking to himself. "I understand what upsets
me," he said. His pie plate had been snatched away
with the table. I supposed that's what upset him. Man
is what he eats, I thought irrelevantly, and, somehow,
the food and wine on the floor seemed to make sense,
to explain the murderous affection of Kramer and
Berliner, the astounded look on Terry's face. "What?"
I said, as if I were more interested in Terry's mind
than in the spectacle of Kramer and Berliner sprawled
in the mess of plates, bottles, glasses, knives, forks,
salmon head, chicken bones, wine. All in all, disgusting, yet happy in lights and colors, especially
with the two of them laughing and hugging. Cavanaugh grinned down at them with contempt. He'd
witnessed better fights, apparently. Paul tried to
smile, but for him the violence was unpleasant and

his smile looked sickly. Canterbury watched my eyes because I was the only one standing. He looked for what to think about this event, but I couldn't tell him anything and I looked down at my feet, where I saw my plate in three pieces, half-moon and two jagged triangles. I wondered if they could be glued together again. Like Kramer and Berliner. No longer rolling, they lay flopped against one another, both wheezing and sweaty. I wondered if it was time for me to go home. Then Terry said, "I'll phone her," and I realized what had upset him. Talking about Deborah, he'd begun to miss her. I said, "Tell her you want to return her earrings."

"Good idea. I'll need some kind of opener." He seemed truly grateful.

"What will you say if you get the answering machine?"

"I won't get it. She's waiting for my call. I can feel it, how she's waiting. I'm glad I talked about her. I wouldn't have understood myself otherwise. I should call her this minute."

"It's 3 a.m.," said Paul. "Give her another half hour. She might like to sleep."

"She never sleeps. Kramer, where's your phone?"

"Don't do it," said Kramer, sitting up to plead. "Don't phone her now."

"Why not?"

"You'll depress me. Phone her tomorrow. You're with us, man."

Berliner sat up, too. "I also had a dream, Terry. Let me tell you about it. Don't make any phone calls. Like Kramer says, you're with us."

Terry considered, then uttered an all-relinquishing sigh. "All right, I'll phone her tomorrow."

It was playacting, this tiny crisis in male sympathy. They seemed to enjoy it, pleading with Terry. Deborah wasn't waiting for his call. He'd said she was never bored. To tease him, I said, "Terry, why don't you do what you feel like doing? Go to the phone. Tell Deborah how you feel, how you miss her keen face that leaps at you. Her voice, her legs. Tell her everything."

"How will I sound?"

"Like a shmuck," said Berliner.

"Who cares?" I said. "Do it."

"Do I want to do it?"

"Certainly. You said so yourself. Go to the phone. Tell her you love her."

"I'll have another glass of wine first."

"You'll never do it, will you?"

"I think you want to do it more than I do."

That felt correct.

"It's late," I muttered, rubbing my chin, feeling bristles. I'd shaved the previous morning. The face is a clock. Other faces also showed the time—slack, negligent flesh, heat in the eyes—but nobody looked ready to quit. "What I mean to say is that, when you talk about Deborah, you sound as if you hate her. You see her in such detail."

"So why should I phone? To tell her I hate her?"

"No. Of course not. You couldn't put it that way."

"How should I put it?"

"Tell her you love her."

"Stay up late enough and you'll say almost anything—even the truth. Maybe Deborah has stopped waiting for my phone call. It's been ten years since I last saw her."

"Ten years?"

"I told you we met shortly after my divorce."

"You still think about her."

"To you, my story sounded bad. Well, it's probably unwise to look too closely at anyone. Who can survive scrutiny? But the woman was unique. A goddess."

"Do you mean that?"

"No. Fatigue makes me sentimental. It's a muscular phenomenon. But I've often considered phoning her. I want to apologize. Put things right."

"So phone her."

"You think I should?"

"I think you can't end an affair with a kick under the table."

"That's a good point."

Cavanaugh kicked open the swinging door to the kitchen, saying, "Jesus Christ," and returned a moment later, kicking the door open from the kitchen side, saying, "What assholes." A new bottle of wine and two water glasses were in his hands. He gave one glass to Terry. He didn't think it was time to go home. I was still standing, wondering if I wanted to phone Deborah Zeller. It seemed almost possible, but what could I say to her? Kramer and Berliner, sitting on the floor beside one another, leaned against a wall. Berliner looked up at Terry and said, "I had a dream about the paper lady. Where I buy my paper every morning."

"Is that so?" said Terry.

"Yeah. The paper lady is fat and stupid. Wears flowery dresses like she floats and doesn't stink. She sits on a high stool holding a cigar box full of change. You can't see the stool, only her lap and legs, she's so fat. Her ankles hang over the tops of her shoes."

"You've made a close study of her."

Berliner considered this and said, "I never thought so before. You know, it's weird. There's a woman in my office who is very pretty, but I couldn't tell you the color of her eyes. The paper lady's eyes are green-ish, full of water. They look sticky. She whistles when she breathes. She has long hairs on her chin. She can't say more than three, four words at a time. Nothing moves except her eyes and fingers making change. She doesn't see good, so she feels the coins. Her heat is in the nickels and dimes. It's like touching her when you take them. I dreamed about her."

"A nightmare," said Terry.

"Once—before the dream—I came for my morning paper and stood reading the front page. I was going to buy the paper, but I was just standing there reading the front page. She says, 'Hey you. This is no library.' There were some other people around and they looked at me like I was trying to cheat the paper lady. I got so pissed, I said, 'I buy a paper from you every morning. You lost a good customer.' I walked away."

Smiling at himself, Berliner continued. "But I was back the next morning. Like, it was more trouble to buy the paper somewhere else, and I wasn't going to let her do this to me. So I went back and stood a minute reading the front page. Not reading. Looking at it, waiting for her to say something. She didn't. So I bought the paper. I don't know who was the winner, but in the dream she was sitting on her stool and I was on my knees, reaching up her dress. On my knees, man, reaching up to the heat. She was letting me. Like not noticing. The most exciting dream I ever had."

As Berliner talked, his eyes seemed to bloat and throb, becoming wet, about to cry. Kramer put his arm around Berliner's shoulders and said, "Yeah, it's weird. Weird."

"I'll tell you what's weird," said Berliner. "What's weird is fucking Terry kills Deborah. Fucking Cavanaugh is turned on by his wife screaming in a blanket. And you, man, you're the weirdest. You lick your table."

"So what, Solly? What's it to you? I get off licking my table."

"Makes me jealous."

Berliner was joking, but also annoyed, maybe miserable. Something in him was difficult to show. Difficult also not to show. Paul, between Terry and Canterbury, the table tipped over in front of them, said, "Hey, since we're talking about tables, I'll tell you about my mother-in-law." His face seemed to hurry, pushing words. "When she eats, you have to wonder if it's a human thing. I stare at her. I lose my appetite. Last night during dinner she was like abolishing a bowl of soup. The noise was revolting. I was staring. She noticed. She stops. 'Paul,' she says. 'Let me live.'"

"Why did you think of that?" asked Terry.

"Your story about Deborah. I think she liked you."

"She stuck her fork in my dessert."

"It was a message. She didn't want to say anything in front of the other doctors. It was a hint."

"Have you been watching me eat?"

"No, man. Hey, Terry, you know about bodies. Tell me something. Could my mother-in-law have extra nerves in her mouth?"

"I'm not a nerve specialist. What did you say to your mother-in-law?"

"I said I was sorry. She lives with us. She's happy when she slobs down a meal. I don't want to inhibit her or anything."

"You know what gets me," said Berliner. "Not important, but I want to say it. Quentin's wife didn't phone. Didn't write a note. Nothing. She doesn't like me, but what the hell. It's not hard to pick up the phone. Quentin was my friend. He would have phoned me if she dropped dead. Men play by the rules, you dig. He was my friend. I lost him and she didn't even tell me."

"I'm sorry, man," said Kramer, squeezing Berliner's shoulder, then withdrawing his arm from around him. "I understand what you feel."

I said, "I have a colleague named Shulman who says that. He interrupts my sentences to name what I feel. Always nodding yes, yes, like he sees a feeling coming. Wants to welcome it, give it a name."

Kramer giggled and said, "I hear you, man."

"I don't think Shulman really resembles you. It's only that he says 'I understand what you feel.' One day he comes up to me outside my office and says, 'Could I have a moment with you? Could I ask you a question?' I said, 'Of course.' He says, 'I heard something you said about me.' I was surprised. Shulman is colorless. There's not much to say about him. To mention his name is to kill conversation. Once I dropped in on him to return a book I'd borrowed. He lives alone near the freeway, two-bedroom house with

a dead lawn out front and a sick plum tree in the
middle of it. He'd just put dinner on the table. The
smell was thick and moist, as if I'd walked into his
bathroom while he was taking a shower. Liver and
boiled potatoes were steaming on the table. It made
me feel sick. Beside the plate was a glass of milk.
That also sickened me. What's to say about Shulman?
He is a thin man who looks like he has heavy organs;
his intestines were shipped to him from Mars, where
the gravitational pull is stronger. I said, 'What did
you hear I said about you?' He says, 'It isn't important. I was hurt.' I said, 'Shulman, tell me what
you heard.' He says, 'I shouldn't have mentioned it.'
He walked away. I told my wife about the incident.
She said, 'Take him to lunch. Talk it over with him.'
I said, 'You think I want to have lunch with that jerk?'
She says, 'See? You called him a jerk. I don't blame
him for feeling hurt.' After that, Shulman began passing me in the hall without saying hello. You know
how it feels when a colorless jerk begins ignoring you?
I began peeking out of my office before I left it, to
make sure he wasn't in the hall. I never before even
thought about Shulman and now I was worried that I
might meet him in the men's room, have to stand
beside him at the urinals. I slipped in and out of my
office like a thief. Then one day I saw him on campus,

same path I was walking, his back to me. I thought of giving him a chance to get far ahead, out of sight. He was hunched, tired-looking. Shorter than I remembered. He was walking slowly, going home to eat liver. As he passed a grove of eucalyptus trees, I saw how tall and healthy the trees looked, as if they didn't give a damn about Shulman. I had to do something. Put an end to this. I called out his name. With enthusiasm. He stops, turns. I was only fifty feet away, but he squints, reaches for his glasses, and his foot catches in the pavement where there is no crack or depression, and he stumbles, loses his glasses. They smashed. I came up to him stammering, 'I'm, I'm . . .' He looks at me and says, 'I understand what you feel.' "

Kramer, giggling again, said, "That's a real funny story, man." Then he got up from the floor, saying, "I have an idea. You'll love this. I'm a genius for thinking of it."

He was heading for the living room, then crossing the orange rug toward a low table, heavily lacquered wood, shaped like a pumpkin. He bent at the table, slid open a drawer. "Here it is."

He turned with a long flat box in his hands, holding it toward us, opening it as he came back. He was smiling hard, as if to demonstrate the only possible reaction to this box. It contained knives, about a dozen slender knives, lying side by side. A narrow elastic belt held them against black plush. Blue handles. Silver blades. They also seemed to smile.

"I won them in Okinawa playing poker with some Marines. Handmade throwing knives. Perfect balance. Feel them. Let's move a little."

"It's nighttime," I said.

"So?"

"Dark outside."

"Fuck that. We'll throw in here. At the kitchen door. Stand up, Harold."

Canterbury leaped from his chair. Ready. Not to throw knives, maybe, but ready to oblige. Berliner was on his feet, too, rolling up his sleeves. He wanted to throw knives. Then Paul and Terry rose. Cavanaugh, last to move, groaned, pressed himself upward. Paul took this moment to retrieve his bag of grass. It had been flung when the table tipped, landing against the wall where Berliner was sitting. Paul looked at it while Berliner spoke and then while I spoke, but he didn't move to get it. I watched him now as he picked up the clear plastic bag, blackened with wine, dripping. He shook it, then cleaned it with a napkin. There was wine inside, too, coagulating lumps of grass. He put the bag with his jacket on the chair he'd been sitting in. Important to him, this good grass, but he hadn't gone after it until the talk was suspended. He didn't now complain about its condition. He'd told us how he apologized to his mother-in-law. It was late and I was a little drunk, feeling a sloppiness of the heart. For whatever it's worth, it struck me that Paul was the nicest man in the room. Kramer, handing out knives, said, "You first, Cavanaugh."

Cavanaugh stood for a moment, knife in hand, looking across the knocked-over table and the mess of fish bones, pastry, and broken glass. The kitchen door, his target, had a long rectangular spruce panel in the center and a redwood border. The spruce was stained dark brown.

"Are you serious, Kramer?"

"Throw it, man."

The knife hit the door, boomed, bounced right, leaving a gouge near the middle. Like an eye. Torn. Weeping splinters.

"Now Paul goes," said Kramer.

Paul raised the knife to his ear, held it for long seconds, staring at a very particular spot, then threw. The knife stuck in the wall to the left of the door. He gasped, hurrying to the knife, and plucked it out of the wall, trailing plaster dust, leaving a slash in the red paper. He rubbed the edges of the slash together, trying to smooth it away. "Sorry, Kramer. Maybe I don't have good aim."

"Canterbury," said Kramer. "You go now."

"I've never done this before."

"Just throw it."

Canterbury raised the knife slowly, pale fingers at the tip of the blade, and threw it, not aiming. The knife made a silvery-blue wheel in the air, hit the center of the door, and stuck, shuddering. The spruce panel was hollow, but there was no boom. His throw had been perfect.

Canterbury put his hands in his trouser pockets and, apologetically, said, "I've never done this before."

"You're a natural," said Kramer. "You're good."

Terry's knife flew like a lead pipe, bashing the door, leaving a channel as long as the blade near the border.

My knife stuck, shivered, fell to the floor.

Berliner threw hardest of anyone. His knife stuck at an angle. "I could kill," he said. "Give me another knife."

Canterbury's second throw was also perfect. We cheered. He smiled in a way that could pass for happiness, showing most of his teeth. Kramer didn't throw any knives. He picked them up after we'd all thrown, and returned them to us, urging us to throw

again. After a while, he didn't have to urge. A rhythm
set in, though we were throwing out of turn, two at a
time, then two or three at a time. The air was full of
steel. The door was gouged and shredded. There was
a lot of grunting, wheezing, and more cheers for Canterbury. He seemed, without really trying, incapable
of a bad throw. His face became pink and vibrant as
he said, "I missed my calling in life."

Knives were chasing each other across the dining
room, booming, bashing against the door, rarely sticking. They bounced away, clattering along the floor
or flying into the side of the dish cabinet. One of
Terry's heavy throws bounced up and chipped the
ceiling. Berliner whooshed a knife into the wall. The
door seemed torn by monstrous fangs. Little remained
to make a solid target. In places the spruce was completely smashed away and I could see through into
the kitchen. Canterbury, high on his success, began
to babble.

"Usually, about this time," he said, "I'm in my
back yard, in robe and slippers, beating my dog with
a magazine. He howls when he hears sirens. Every
dog in the neighborhood howls when he does. I'd get
rid of him, but he's a gift. An oil man sent him to me
from Alaska. Part malamute, part wolf. Enormously
impressive animal, but there are sirens almost every

night. He howls with ghastly authenticity. I expect to
be sued one day."

"It's not ghastly," said Cavanaugh, lowering his
knife. There was nothing but splinters and holes to
throw at. Terry and Berliner were sitting again. "I
used to play summer ball with a team called the Red
Wolves. Semi-pro league. When we won a game, the
team howled in the locker room, all the players and
the coach. It was fine." He tipped his head back,
neck muscles swelling as he pulled in air through
funneled lips, hunched his shoulders, and howled:
"*Ow-oo-ooo, ow-woo-oo-ooo.*"

"Neat," said Canterbury. A white smile cut the
gloomy face neatly. He tipped his head back, stretch-
ing the slender pipe of his neck, and howled as if
yearning after Cavanaugh's howl, catching its final
note, winding it higher, higher, and higher toward
sublimity. Berliner, with lunatic enthusiasm, came
wailing after Canterbury. The three of them were
howling together. Terry joined with a bellowing howl
and then Paul started yipping hysterically. Now all
five were doing it, harmoniously overlapping, layer-
ing the air with howls.

The ceiling was chipped, the wall beside the door
torn, bleeding dusty gas. The dish cabinet carried
zigzag gashes down one side. The kitchen door was

splinters and the hardwood floor was streaked with wiry lines where blades had skated.

When I howled I felt the vibrations in my head, way up around the sinuses, but I couldn't hear myself too well. I could hear Kramer, though. Everyone could hear Kramer. Wonderful notes evolved from his darkness. Magnificent tears came down from his eyes.

The howling was liquid, long, and thick in the red room, heart of Kramer's house. His cherished table lay on its side like a dead beast, stiff-legged and eviscerated, streaming crockery, silver, wine, meat, bones, and broken glass. We sounded lost, but I thought we'd found ourselves. I mean nothing psychological. No psycho-logic of the soul, only the mind, and this was mindless. The table's treasure lay spilled and glittering at our feet and we howled, getting better at it as the minutes passed, entering deeply into our sound, and I felt more and more separated from myself, closer to the others, until it seemed we were one in the rising howls, rising again and again, taking us up even as we sank toward primal dissolution, assenting to it with this music of common animality, like a churchly chorus, singing of life and death.

Kramer quit howling and said, "I'll clean up tomorrow," which made me turn toward the living room, following his eyes and voice. A woman stood on the orange rug, near the open footlocker, among Kramer's snapshots, his hundreds of other women. We all stopped howling. She glanced from face to face, then to the debris, tracing knife lines through lakes of wine, searching for a theme in too many clues, and then said, "Tonight," as if he had said that.

He said it: "Tonight."

Berliner howled. Nobody joined him. He quit, grinned, said, "Hi, Nancy."

"Hi, Solly."

"We'll help clean up," said Paul. "No trouble, Nancy. Come on, men."

Nobody moved.

She had a small, tipped-up nose. Soft pointy mouth. Cartoon simplicity. Conventionally pretty. Her voice belonged to another face, older, complicated by experience, not so pretty. I wondered if Kramer had photographed her.

She wore a blue-green blouse; lank, slick material, open to the second button, hanging over the top of her jeans. No bra. Free, indifferent; sexy, but more like self-possessed. The slick material trembled with her breathing. Watery effects. Nothing else showed her distress.

Dark blond hair, parted in the middle, was brushed back toward her ears. Her forehead was high; eyes widely spaced, oval, brown, clearly receptive. They challenged Kramer with patient staring. No judgments in them; she simply expected him to speak. He said, "Hey, you had your hair cut, didn't you? Looks good. Very very good."

"I like it, too," said Paul.

"Thanks."

"The horizontal look," said Kramer. "It's in. Very in. One of my clients had her hair cut for the vertical look. The same day she sees a magazine cover and the model's hair is altogether fucking opposite hers. She goes vertical, the world goes horizontal. It really bothered her. Made her feel stupid. Vertical when everybody is horizontal. She went deaf for a week."

"Do you think it's fair talking about her this way?"

"Yeah. Where did you have it cut? San Francisco?"

"A woman friend cut it for me."

"Good job. What do you call it—layered, right? Sort of a windblown look. Like a beach. Windy beach. Your friend knows what she's doing. My client paid eighty bucks to get her hair cut, then talked about it with me. Another fifty bucks. Figure a hundred and thirty bucks for a haircut, plus going deaf. She could hear the phone ring, but no voices. Went deaf to voices. Told me people were screaming at her—husband, kids, even the clerks in the supermarket. I had to laugh. Not in front of her, naturally. She was too freaked out. I went to the toilet, shut the door. I laughed and laughed."

I supposed it was a funny story, but didn't laugh. Neither did anyone else. Kramer, suddenly an impetuous talker, was deaf to himself. Nancy moved before he finished, stepping through the confusion of the dining-room floor. She was wearing sandals. Pretty feet. I imagined her ankles and legs were also pretty and I began to look for imperfections. Do women look at each other this way? It felt indecent, in these circumstances, but I couldn't not do it. If she were perfect, I'd feel depressed. At the dish cabinet, she stopped, looked at the gashes down one side, touched them lightly with her fingertips.

"Oh, I'll get rid of those marks," said Kramer very confidently, almost boasting. She wasn't listening. He shut up and watched her. She pushed the splintered door, entered the kitchen. We heard the refrigerator seal breaking with a gasp. After a few seconds, the door shut. "You must have been hungry," she said. Her voice, coming from the kitchen, had nothing special in it beyond this observation.

"Yeah," said Kramer, echoing her tone, "we were starving. I'll replace the food tomorrow. I'll have it catered—chicken, salmon, everything. What time is your women's group coming over?"

He faced the kitchen door, hands on his hips. He looked ready. Weight evenly distributed, head up, glance fixed on the door. Ready to listen, answer, act. The door opened. Nancy reentered the dining room. "I feel invaded."

"Right," said Kramer, as if she'd answered his question precisely. "I hear you and I want to think about what you're saying. Invaded. What do you feel about that?"

Berliner giggled. "Why don't you put it on tape?"

Kramer glanced at him as if the idea were considerable.

"Put it on tape," said Nancy. "Maybe you'll want to play it back later while you're thinking about it."

Kramer nodded. "You mean it would like tell me something about our relationship?" He was ready for that, too. Very agreeable. Ready to learn. It came to me that, for Kramer, life was forever open to new understandings. Amid the destruction of his dining room, he was committed to no particular interpretation of anything.

"All this is telling me something about our relationship," she said.

"Sure, baby. That's what we've been talking about the whole night. Relationships."

"Hi, Nancy," said Cavanaugh.

"Hi, Cavanaugh."

We'd remained where she found us, Kramer closest to her, at the edge of the spill, the toppled dining-room table approximately between them, slightly to her right.

"Let's go sit in the living room," said Kramer. "I'll turn on the machine. You say what you feel."

She nodded the way he did. "The feeling machine."

Kramer smiled. She didn't.

"I can say what I feel without the machine, but I feel—even saying this—you might feel I'm cutting your balls off. I sense negative vibes. You feel I'm like ruining your party, don't you?"

"I don't know about that. But you aren't responsible for my feelings. We have discussed this, right? I mean I could feel what I feel and you could feel—"

"Right, right, right. I understand. I appreciate your feelings about your freedom and being a creative person."

"And I appreciate how you, like, want to express yourself."

"But you feel I don't have to do it this minute. I could express myself later."

"It could be later," said Kramer, generosity in his voice, accepting her idea as if he were offering her something.

"I mean I understand how it could be later. That's cool." She nodded again in his manner as she spoke, same generous ingratiating tone as his. "Sure, it could be later. We could sit down later. Talk."

They looked at each other, nodding, birdlike, a ritual dance of species recognition. The rest of us looked at them. Their unanimity made us seem disorganized and irrelevant: marginal men, incidental scribbles. Even the giant Cavanaugh looked trivial compared to them. Yet I wondered if, in a room full of men and women, I could have guessed Kramer was married to this woman. Probably not. I expect physical similarities. Not the familiar fat of conjugal loneliness or the clumsy compulsive first person plural, but something in the original beings, their racial teleology, similarities in hair, eyes, shape of lip and foot. It's as if, in couples, I expect cows or gorillas. Never the unpredictable discrepancies of a human man and woman. No, I couldn't have guessed these two were married. He had luxuriously fashioned black hair; and his arms, tattooed in blue and red, seemed to spring from his soul. She was simple, immediately present. No costume instinct, plainly pretty in color and bone; nothing to hide or advertise. He was dark, she light. His expression was sensuous, a mix of menace and self-love, qualified by his eye problem, the way he blinked occasionally to focus. Her expression was neutral, consistent, what you sometimes see in good-looking women—facial restraint, close to deadness, as if they fear their effect on others. They looked chemically antithetical. Not right. All wrong. But love is blind, unreasonable—forget plausible— and marriages are made in heaven. Kramer was insanely reasonable now. "Yeah, we could sit down, have a cup of coffee, talk. In the morning, like."

"It is the morning."

This was sharp contradiction, or qualification. Kramer assimilated it quickly. "Right," he said, cocking his head, snapping his fingers, then back to hands on hips. Ready once more. I was on his side, though it was hard to root for him; something in his will to accommodate was contemptible. Besides, she was prettier; perhaps smarter, but I couldn't tell about that because she had a certain moral advantage, given the circumstances. The way her blouse continued trembling also affected my sympathies, making pity and sadism masturbate each other, making me like her, and, even without better evidence than I had, making me wonder if Kramer deserved this woman. She said, "What you are saying is that we could wait until the sun comes up. Is that, like, what you mean?"

I heard faint pressure on the "like" and realized, for the first time, she was imitating Kramer. A form of praise, imitation works also for hate. Nothing substantially personal had been said, yet hearing even this was a privileged, if awkward, intimacy. Some couples relish public battle; these two had style; manners; almost Japanese in their gracious distance.

"Yeah," said Kramer, "that's what I mean. We

could wait till the sun comes up. But I don't want to do some oppressive fascist number on you. I mean if you would like to talk now, I could dig it."

"But you would like to talk when the sun comes up. That's fine with me. I like to talk when the sun comes up. It's more creative."

Kramer thought for a second, then said, "Yeah," nodding. She joined him, both nodding, as if toward a truth beyond themselves, extremely general and creative. Then she turned, went into the kitchen, disappeared, reappeared, ruined door flying with her passing through it toward Kramer, who stood hands on hips, nodding, nodding, watching her come swiftly to him, hands above her head.

One doesn't always see, for an instant, what one sees. This was such blind seeing, as she came, her hands clasped about the thing, coming down with her hands onto Kramer's head at the hairline. Black iron pot struck gonk. Resonance followed. No appreciable damage to Kramer's hair style, but red worms came creeping forth, feeling slowly toward his eyebrows.

I looked at Cavanaugh, as if to see what I'd seen, and found him between surprise and negation—"Oh" and "Don't." Berliner's face, left of Cavanaugh's, showed nothing. Slowed by marijuana, he waited for significance in the act.

Kramer stood dummied, glazed, hands on hips, forehead flashy with blood. He rocked slightly, absorbing the blow, letting force slip down spinal ridges to ass and legs and heels while his hair released blood; red genius, oozing from his mind. He acknowledged no pain, didn't seem to know he was bleeding. Didn't lift a hand to his head. Merely blinked to restore focus. They stood face to face, powerfully coupled, while the rest of us shifted weight, gaping and incapable. Then Kramer spoke:

"I feel you're feeling anger."

Terry muttered, "Half a dozen stitches. Probably not serious, but if there is vomiting later . . ."

"Grounds for divorce," said Canterbury, "assuming the injured spouse survives." He sounded eerily pleased and was smiling. A wide, rash smile. Apparently hysterical; high on the action. Maybe frightened, but pleased by his fear. His smile was gothic.

Nancy said, "I want to express myself, like now."

"I feel you're feeling anger," said Kramer again. "What do you feel about that?"

He was, obviously, trying to evoke her deepest motives. She screamed and brought the pot up from her abdomen, following the same arc as before. Kramer went backwards on his heels to dodge it, stumbling toward the living room, losing balance,

sitting down hard on the edge of the orange rug. She
went after him. Paul leaped out of her way. Cavanaugh grabbed for her and Berliner turned his head
not to look. Cavanaugh's hand, catching her shoulder,
crushed her blouse against the bone. She stopped,
swiveled her head toward the hand. Looked at it, not
him, as if she scrutinized a noxious insect. It let go.
She proceeded to Kramer, bent toward his face, and
said, "I don't want to talk to you."

"Okay," said Kramer, gazing at her knees, not
showing anything or doing anything or conceding anything, but abiding. She straightened, walked past him,
going to the stairs, and, with mechanical trudge, up
the stairs. A door slammed. Opened. Her voice said,
"Tonight. You clean up tonight." Then came a smashing noise against the ceiling directly above our heads.
I remembered she'd carried the pot upstairs. She was
smashing it against the floor, the noise changing as it
smashed a rug, bare boards, a wall, and then came
breaking glass. Then it stopped. We heard sobbing.

Kramer, still sitting on the rug, gazing at nothing,
said, "I don't know what's going on. Never nags,
never complains, never has moods, never even gets
sick, and now she has a tizzy. What the hell is going
on? Man, I thought we had an understanding." He
shook his head abruptly, as you'd shake a bottle to

feel if there's liquid sloshing inside. Blood sprinkled the rug.

Berliner, glancing at the spots on the rug, said, "Anyone can see that."

Paul said quietly, "Let's clean up."

"No," cried Kramer, rising with determination. "You guys shouldn't do that. You're my guests."

Nobody mentioned his face. It was difficult not to stare, not to think how odd that he couldn't see it himself.

"We want to help," said Canterbury. "Terry, take that end of the table. Is there a broom?"

"Kitchen," said Kramer glumly, standing now, suddenly a pointless man, all determination gone. Cavanaugh stepped toward the kitchen. Canterbury and Terry righted the table. Berliner and I squatted at the edge of the mess, plucking out the unbroken things—salad bowl, knives, forks—putting them on the table. Paul joined us. Kramer hovered, watched the work, doing nothing. We'd taken his initiative away, all moving quickly and efficiently, but he was preoccupied, listening for Nancy. There came a sound of water flushing upstairs, again, again, again. Kramer said, "She does that when she's mad, but only sometimes."

"Do you know about the noiseless flush?" said

Canterbury instantly, eager to be pertinent, to advise. "Toilet bowls that make no sound. At most a whisper. I'll give you the name of my plumber."

Berliner said, "I don't like the idea."

Canterbury turned to him. "Why not?"

"Doesn't seem right. If there's no flush, I might forget to flush. Leave turds floating in the bowl."

Flushing persisted upstairs; violent annihilations.

I said, "Let's discuss it."

Canterbury and Berliner smiled at each other. Kramer, half-smiling, tried to join them in spirit. Cavanaugh swept steadily, shoving glass, sticky food, and wine into a glittering heap. Paul crouched beside it with a dustpan. The flushing stopped. I was grateful for the silence. Kramer looked up at the ceiling, as if at clouds that prophesied the weather. Berliner started to say something. Kramer said, "Wait." Berliner shut up. The silence ended with a long thunderous crash. The house shuddered. Dust drifted down from the ceiling. "The Victorian dresser," whispered Kramer. "Big mother. I don't know how she did it. Must be really pissed, really pissed." He looked at us. "What do you think?"

His face, gripped by this question, was so grotesquely sensational nobody could speak to it. Red lines tangled from hair to jaw, some dry, some wet, and black eyes came beating through as if looking for a way out of Kramer's head. He said, "Enough. Enough. I'll do the rest. You guys get out. I'm really glad you came by tonight. The evening means a lot to me. I want to do it again. I'll work out a schedule with Nancy. That's our problem, like. I see it now. We need a better schedule. You all take off now. I swear that dresser weighs half a ton. Marble and oak. She pushed it over, you dig? It's like time for you to go home. She'd never say anything so uncool, but I know her. I see what she's, like, trying to say. If you hang around, it could fuck up my marriage."

Not to see his face as his marriage wasn't easy. I suppressed the metaphor. This was no time for aesthetic reactions. Cavanaugh leaned the broom against the wall.

Kramer put out his hand to me. I stepped forward, shook it affectionately. With dense, frowning doubt, Terry did the same. Canterbury did it, saying, "I'll phone with the name of my plumber." Kramer nodded, "Yeah, yeah." Paul, then Berliner, hugged him. Cavanaugh, arm around Kramer's shoulders, said, "Call me if you need anything. Call any time, man."

Terry said, "You see about the cut there." He gestured vaguely toward Kramer's hairline. Still bleeding.

Kramer urged us with his eyes: goodbye. "Wonder-ful club," he said, focusing on each of us in turn as we moved toward the door. He remained where he stood in the dining room, peering through bloody reticulations, urging, yearning. Then he waved goodbye.

The door shut. We were outside.

We collected under a street lamp, making a circle, a sort of room, with our bodies. Pines stood along the street. I smelled wisteria and roses. No sounds followed us from Kramer's house. Paul drew his bag of grass from his jacket. Wine-clotted. He separated dry pieces slowly. We watched as he rolled a thick, ragged cigarette, bulging in the middle, twisted and pinched at the ends to compensate for the bulge. Can-terbury said, "Nancy's good-looking, isn't she?"

Paul said, "Uhm," and lit the cigarette, dragging hard, then passed it to Berliner. Canterbury tried again: "We can't leave him in there like that, can we?"

Berliner dragged, coughed. "It's where he lives."

He passed the cigarette to me. I took a short drag, passed it to Cavanaugh. He did the same, passing it next to Terry. He studied it for a moment, started to pass it away, but then committed it to his lips. He took in a little smoke, fired it out quickly, passing the cigarette to Canterbury. He made the tip sizzle in a long suck, held the smoke as if he'd done this often before, and forced a smile. His creamy slacks billowed at the cuff. He looked antiseptic, chipper, cheery, frightened—the man didn't have one way to be.

Paul, with the cigarette again, held it close to his lips, looking shrewd, but when he spoke his voice was entirely innocent. "You know what I think? I think that was great. It was like an experience."

Cavanaugh said, "For Kramer."

"For all of us. I'm glad I saw it. I'm glad."

He was massively sincere. Nobody tried to qualify his comment.

Terry said, "I've got to work tomorrow."

"Me, too," I said.

Then Berliner began quietly humming. I looked at him and saw that he'd shut his eyes. His humming flowed into words: "For he's a jolly good fellow . . ."

I know I would have laughed, but Cavanaugh stopped me by joining Berliner, singing in slow, quiet tones, "For he's a jolly good fellow." Together they were irresistible and all of us began doing it, singing in the flowery piney dark outside Kramer's house. When we reached the last line, fourth or fifth time around, "Which nobody can deny," it seemed awesomely true, maybe because of the trees, parked cars, hedges, and houses. These dumb ministers of the street denied nothing and there was no denial even from Kramer's house, though I expected it very much, a shout, a scream, or something worse. We stopped singing. A sudden deep drop to silence. The earth pressed up against my feet.

Cavanaugh looked at Kramer's house, as if for the effect of our voices, but quietude had resumed, cool dark air resumed. "I've got to go," he whispered, not going, and then he raised his voice, "But I'm not sleepy. Man, I don't even want to sleep. I'm going for a drive."

Terry said, "I'm not sleepy either."

Berliner, tentatively, almost shyly, said, "Me neither. I know a breakfast place in San Francisco."

Canterbury said, "Let me buy breakfast for you fellows." He tried to restrain himself, not show us how much he wanted to buy us breakfast, but his voice jumped with enthusiasm and hope, spoiling the idea a little.

I said, "Well, I don't know."

Paul dragged on his marijuana, finishing it, building toward action, and then said, "Let's go in Cavanaugh's pickup," as if the decision to go had been made.

Nobody moved. Berliner checked our faces for objections. Nobody said no. Terry moaned, "I've got to work tomorrow," but that wasn't no. In fact, it was a sort of yes. Berliner nudged Cavanaugh and they took off together, as if with the same place in mind, a great big man and a man with white hair striding together up the street. I lingered, but only until Paul grabbed my arm, pulling me after him. I didn't resist. Terry and Canterbury followed, everyone walking quickly.

The bed of Cavanaugh's pickup was hard on my ass. Also cold to the touch. It rumbled and jounced. Terry and Paul huddled against the back of the cab, talking and laughing. I heard Terry shout, against the noise of the pickup, "I said to her 'I love you,' " and Paul laughed and looked at me. Though I'd missed the story, I laughed, and then, with the pickup building speed along the avenue to the freeway, I couldn't hear a word they were saying. But I laughed and the wind ripped my face; numbing, loud. First light lay along the shore and out along the mud flats of the bay, a cottony glow gathering against black resistance in the morning sky. Cavanaugh pushed hard, ninety or better, going through Emeryville. I could feel his happiness in the speed. Like the new day, despite resistance, being born. "Where are we going?" I screamed. Not for answer; just to scream. The wind ate my question. Terry's bald head dipped toward me. Pale ceramic bulb; it must have been freezing in the wind. He winked. Canterbury's face popped up in the back window of the cab and I noticed, in the exaggerated motion of his lips, he was singing, nodding his head to the beat. As we approached the toll booth to the Bay Bridge, Cavanaugh had to slow down. I could hear them singing inside the cab. Paul and Terry joined in and so did I. We pulled away from the toll booth toward high steel pylons and great sweeping loops of cable, all of us singing of Kramer, jolly good fellow we'd left in his dining room, peering after us, waving goodbye. Jolly good fellow. Which nobody should deny.